Thunder Canyon™

Donald Brewer

A Mouse Gate™ Secret Service Mystery

TotalRecall Publications, Inc.
1103 Middlecreek
Friendswood, Texas 77546
281-992-3131   281-482-5390 Fax
www.totalrecallpress.com

ISBN: 978-1-59095-294-8
UPC: 6-43977-42944-5

Library of Congress Control Number: 2014955304

Printed in the United States of America with simultaneous printings in Australia, Canada, and United Kingdom.

FIRST EDITION
1   2   3   4   5   6   7   8   9   10

TO THE MEMORY OF BOBBY G., A GOOD FRIEND AND MENTOR - NOT TO MENTION ONE-OF-A-KIND.

AUTHOR: DONALD BREWER

Donald Brewer spent 26 years with the United States Secret Service, retiring as the Special Agent-In-Charge of the Counterfeit Division in Washington, D.C. Don spent his early years as an undercover and case agent in the Atlanta Field Office before moving to Miami, where he spent 11 years in the 1980's when Miami was the counterfeit capital of the world. In one 24-month period, he and his squad suppressed 26 counterfeit manufacturing operations. He has appeared on the Discovery Channel and the Learning Channel in episodes detailing the manufacturing of counterfeit U.S. currency. In 1999, he appeared on National Public Radio (NPR) to educate the public on the issuing of the newly designed U.S. Currency. In addition, he has given speeches and made presentations regarding counterfeit U.S. currency at various conferences and seminars sponsored by Interpol and other foreign police agencies.

Don and his wife, Linda are the proud owners of two Peruvian horses (SRR Animoso and LEA Torreon), and have ridden in a number of shows and parades. Don is a throat cancer survivor, and after 12 years, has been declared cured. Such victories do not come without a price; Don now speaks with an electronic artificial larynx. The couple split their time between St. Simons Island, GA, and Cotopaxi, Colorado. They are pictured here with Watson, their English Cocker Spaniel.

The author's first book, Worthy of Trust and Confidence, was one of the three finalists in the Colorado Authors League, Young Adult Book of the Year for 2014. It was also the Grand Prize winner in The Ultimate Heroes Writing Contest, Western Division.

Visit www.DonaldBrewer.com, Like DonBrewerBooks on Facebook

ACKNOWLEDGMENT

I would like to thank Mike Sampson, the USSS Archivist, for photos and historical information. I would also like to thank Andre' and Sandy, for their reading, editing, and photography. A special thanks to Mary Beth for the genuine, Irish Shillelagh, which was brought to the U.S. by her grandmother in the 1930's. Thanks also to my wife, Linda, for her typing, editing and continued support.

About the Book

This book is unusual, since it deals with the counterfeiting of gold coins and gold bars circa 1900. Most Americans, outside of coin collectors, don't realize that gold coins were once a common form of currency in our country. In the book is a photo of a counterfeit gold coin detector, patented in 1857, that depicts spaces for 1 dollar, 2.5 dollar, 3 dollar, 5 dollar, 10 and 20 dollar gold coins. The book is set in 1900; Cripple Creek, Colorado, a gold "boom town." It details a Secret Service Investigation of a counterfeit gold coin and bar operation.

List of Characters

Maggie, Stephen and Lizzie – The trio of cousins who are given the magical gold coin that unlocks the Mousegate.

Eddie Donnally - Secret Service Operative sent to conduct a counterfeit coin and gold bar case in the gold mine boom town of Cripple Creek, Colorado, in 1900.

An Li - Secret Service Operative and partner of Eddie Donnally.

Mary Helen MacDougal - Manager of the Haven House, Cripple Creek, Colorado, a charity and home for single ladies and children.

Kira Cassidy and her brothers - a family of counterfeiters.

J.T. Raines - partner of Kira Cassidy in the counterfeit conspiracy, and crooked owner of the Wild Horse Saloon and gambling hall.

PROLOGUE

Jeremiah Klein leaned against the bar and savored his whisky. Jeremiah did odd jobs and made deliveries for a couple of local tough guys. Life was good, at least right now. He had pinched five gold coins from a package he delivered and mistakenly believed no one had noticed.

"Hello, Jerry," said Bill Braxton, who had a slight New York accent. Braxton was prone to shortening everyone's name.

Jerry turned and stared. He hadn't seen Braxton come in.

"You doing alright, Jeremiah?" he heard from the other side, receiving a sharp clap on the back. John Powell, another local thug, had slid up on the other side. Both men were much bigger than Klein and towered over him in very menacing stances.

Jeremiah Klein made a lot of deliveries for Braxton and Powell.

"You shouldn't have pinched some of those $10 gold eagles Jerry," hissed Braxton.

"I'm sorry fellas. You know I've never done anything like that before," stammered Jeremiah.

"We know, Jeremiah. That's why we are going to take it easy on you," said Powell. "Did you give any of the eagles to anyone else?"

"No. I swear," said Klein, lying through his teeth. "I spent them all."

"Well, since you've done so good in the past, the boss told us to go easy on you," said Braxton.

"You're getting out of town," said Powell.

Klein was speechless.

"The boss told us to escort you back to Leadville and give you one hundred dollars to go anywhere you want - East or West," advised Braxton.

Jerry's relief was obvious. "When are we going?" he asked.

"Right now," said Powell.

"But my clothes and stuff are at the boarding house," whined Klein.

"Don't worry, Jerry. With the one hundred bucks, you can buy new stuff," said Braxton.

Braxton and Powell joked with Klein to keep him at ease as they walked to the Midland Terminal. Klein relaxed and was not alarmed at the situation. The trio caught the Rio Grande train headed for Leadville.

Halfway through the trip, Braxton said, "Come on, Jerry. Let's go get some grub and a drink."

"I'm not hungry," said Klein, "but a drink sounds good."

The train was crossing a high trestle over a spot called Ghost Canyon. The dynamite booms from the mines were almost continuous due to the echoes. As they entered the area between two cars, Braxton turned and gave Klein a wicked punch to the stomach. With Klein bent over, Powell and Braxton grabbed him by the shirt and seat of his pants and threw him off the train. Klein's screams were covered by the booms of the dynamite blasts.

"Guess there will be one more ghost in the Canyon tonight," laughed Braxton.

"Let's go get that drink," said Powell. "Killing always makes me thirsty."

CHAPTER 1

The three cousins gaited up to the secluded spring.

"I can't believe that Nicky Adams," fumed Maggie. "Carrying on about her Tennessee Walker and how smooth his gait is."

"I know," said Stephen. "Our Peruvians are smoother and can cover more ground than any of those Walkers. I've run her horse into the ground several times. Her dad even complained to Abuelo."

They dismounted and let the horses drink. It was a beautiful fall day in Tennessee, with the trees in full color.

"Uh, guys," said Lizzie, pulling a glowing gold coin and chain out from under her shirt.

"My turquoise nugget is getting warm," exclaimed Maggie.

Stephen pulled a Secret Service badge out of his pocket, and it too was glowing. "These mementos from our last adventure can only be seen by us, Mimi and Abuelo."[1]

"I think we better get back to Mimi," said Maggie, climbing on her horse.

The trio gaited back three miles to the barn on Mimi and

---

[1] ***Author's Note:*** *To learn more about their mementos, see 'Worthy of Trust and Confidence', a Mouse Gate Series Book, by this author.*

Abuelo's recently expanded 80-acre spread. Their place backed up to a large state park that was laced with horse trails. In fact, that was the reason Mimi and Abuelo had bought their place. The horses were in good shape, so they made it home quickly.

"Let's just put them in the stalls," suggested Maggie. "We can un-tack them after we check with Mimi."

The trio ran to the back door and started calling for Mimi as soon as they got inside.

Mimi was sitting on a sofa in the great room. Sitting across from her was Ace. Once again, the little leprechaun was dressed in jeans, cowboy boots and wearing a four-leaf clover bolo.

"Top of the morning," said Ace, touching the brim of his hat with his shillelagh, and giving them a wide grin.

"You guys want some lemonade?" asked Mimi.

"Of course," the youngsters replied in unison.

"Don't commit yourselves to anything with Ace until I get back," she instructed.

"How bout a wee dram of the Irish for me?" asked Ace.

"Okay," said Mimi. "You know where it is. Help yourself to a wee dram."

The little man went over to a cabinet and poured himself a half glass of single malt Irish whisky and held it up to the light admiringly. He turned to the trio, who were now on the sofa. "I may have a new adventure for you; that is, if you're interested," tempted the leprechaun.

The three started to talk at once, but Maggie held up her hand. "We read Eddie's journal after we came back, but it didn't give us a real ending. I'd like to hear how things turned out."

"Well, I don't usually talk outside of the journals, but I believe I can make an exception for you three," said Ace, giving them a conspiratorial wink.

"Will and Lisa had a big wedding in Texas. It was quite the grand affair. I can tell you that," said Ace.

"Did you go? And, what happened after that?" asked Lizzie, the youngest, but the most romantic of the group.

"Sorry, lassie, but that's the best I can do, without going into another journal," answered Ace.

"Have you got another journal for us, Ace?" asked Stephen.

"Aye, I do," said Ace, "well, not exactly a journal."

"Hold up, Ace," warned Mimi, returning with the lemonade.

Ace sneaked a quick swallow of the whisky.

Once Mimi was settled back on the sofa, she said, "Ace has a trip to tell you about, but it is not the same as before. He operates as a sort of guardian angel for certain people, including our family, among others. Although, I hesitate to call him an angel - devil is usually more like it."

"That's cool," answered the three kids excitedly.

"Go ahead, Ace," ordered Mimi. "Tell them."

"Well, its like this . . . Eddie Donnally is in a wee spot of trouble, and he could use a hand," said the leprechaun.

"What kind of trouble?" asked Maggie.

"He's working on a counterfeit gold coin and gold bar case, and he and his partner are out-on-a-limb by themselves," answered Ace.

"Why don't you help him?" asked Stephen, sarcastically. "You seem to have plenty of magic."

"Oh, laddie, one of these days, I am going to give you a taste of me shillelagh," declared Ace. "It doesn't work that way. I can send someone, but I cannot go me self."

"So what do you want us to do, Mr. Ace?" asked Lizzie politely.

Mimi held up a hand. "This is a whole different trip than what you went on before. There is no journal about where you are going. That happens when it's a guardian angel trip. There is no previous record of what you're getting into or how it ends."

The trio looked at each other. "Does that mean we are going as ourselves?" asked Maggie.

"Aye," said Ace. "This time you won't be seeing history. You will be making history!" He held his glass up in a salute.

Mimi squirmed on the sofa. "This is a dangerous thing," she said. "But, Ace believes you three can help Eddie and keep him and his partner safe."

"Jeez," said Stephen. "From the last journal, Eddie Donnally seems like the last person who would need our help."

"You're not kidding!" added Maggie.

"Trust me," said Ace, looking each of them in the eyes. "I wouldn't ask you to do this if I didn't think you were up to it."

The three turned to Mimi. "What do you say Mimi?" asked Maggie.

"I've known Ace a long time, and I do trust him, relatively speaking. So, I am okay with you going," she answered. "But, I've already threatened his "wee" life if one of you gets hurt."

"I'll be looking after them in me own way," answered Ace, solemnly. "You have my word, Mimi."

"You three go tend to the horses and turn them out, while I go over a few details with Ace," instructed Mimi.

CHAPTER 2

While they un-tacked the horses, the trio talked non-stop.

"I'm a little scared," said Lizzie. "I don't think I've ever seen Mimi so serious."

"You're right," said Stephen. "Did you notice how Ace called her Mimi? That's our family's pet name for her. I thought we were the only ones who called her that. I bet she's in there laying down the law."

"I noticed it too," said Maggie. "And, that makes me believe she's known Ace a long, long time, and trusts him, more or less."

"I really enjoyed what we did before, so I'm ready for something more," said Stephen, pulling out his Secret Service badge and rubbing it.

"Me too," said Maggie, touching the turquoise nugget under her shirt. "You don't have to go, Lizzie, if you don't want to."

"Are you kidding? I'm not letting you two have all the fun," said Lizzie.

"Well, let's go tell Mimi and Ace," said Maggie.

When they got back inside, Ace was gone and Mimi was still on the sofa.

"Ace left this for you," said Mimi, holding up a $10 dollar Gold Eagle coin. "You can carry it, Lizzie. No one can see it but us."

"Where is the Mousegate this time?" asked Stephen.

"Where do you think?" asked Mimi, rolling her eyes.

"Yeah, we're going back to Disney World," squealed Lizzie.

"I'll tell the family I've decided on a quick Thanksgiving trip to Disney World for anybody that wants to go," said Mimi.

"Where's Abuelo?" asked Stephen.

"He went trout fishing with his friend Stan. He'll be back before long," answered Mimi. "He'll go with us, of course."

"Last time we wandered all over the park. Did Ace tell you exactly where it is this time, Mimi?" asked Stephen.

"No," answered Mimi. "I've asked him before, but for some reason, Ace never seems to know. At least that's what he says."

"It must be some kind of stupid leprechaun rule," laughed Stephen.

"Don't think I didn't hear that, laddie," they all heard Ace's lilting Irish voice fill the room.

Everyone laughed, but Stephen, who blushed, said, "Sorry, Ace," to no one in particular.

CHAPTER 3

It was a crisp, early fall day in Washington, D.C. Eddie Donnally was heading for the Secret Service Headquarters when a newspaper headline at a newsstand just outside the building caught his eye.

"Former Secretary of the Treasury to Prison"

Eddie fished ten cents out of his pocket as the newsstand vendor turned toward him.

"Hello, Freddie," said Donnally.

"Hey, Mr. Donnally. How's New York?" asked the vendor.

"It's good. I get to be around the family and all that," laughed Eddie.

"I know exactly," laughed the vendor. "You know what they say, you can pick your friends, but you're stuck with your family. Is that one of your cases?" he asked, pointing to the news headline.

"Not really," said Eddie. "That was Will Scott's last case."

"I heard he got married and was living out West. That Pinky McFadden was buying everyone drinks at the Pub once he heard the news that Scott wasn't coming back," informed the man laughing.

"A lot of us went out to the wedding," said Eddie. "It was a lot of fun. His wife, Lisa, is a gem and quite a pretty lass. The only thing wrong with her is she's not Irish."

"Are you back for good?" asked Freddie.

"No, I've got a meeting with the new Chief. I've got to run or I'll be late," replied Eddie, tucking the newspaper under his arm and striding quickly into the building.

"Top of the morning, Doris," beamed Eddie at the Chief's secretary. Doris was on her third Chief.

She stood up and gave Eddie a hug. He was so surprised, he almost dropped his newspaper.

"I've missed you and all your foolishness," confessed the woman.

Recovering his composure, Eddie asked, "Did you see the paper?"

"No. I heard though," answered Doris.

"Here, take a look while I see the Chief," said Eddie, handing her the paper.

Eddie found his partner, An Li, regaling the Chief with their latest case in New York.

"You know you can't believe a thing he says, John," Eddie chimed in addressing the Chief. "I'm sorry, I mean Chief."

"Shut up, Eddie, and don't you call me Chief, at least not in here," answered John Bell, the newly appointed eighth Chief of the U.S. Secret Service. "Every time somebody calls me Chief, I look around to see who they're talking to. Chief Taylor will always be Chief to me."

"How's he doing out there in Denver?" asked Eddie.

"Loving life, he says," answered Bell.

After breaking up a counterfeit ring that included two cabinet secretaries, Chief Taylor had prophesized his retirement. The politicians all publicly applauded him and the Service, but privately a number of them squirmed. All of a sudden, Chief Taylor was an outsider that nobody quite trusted. After a couple of funding disputes, the Chief and Miss Lucy, his wife, headed for Denver. The Chief had sent Eddie Donnally back to New York right after the case. Eddie was just too well-known around Washington.

"I've been in New York for over two years, and please tell me you're not bringing us back here," said Eddie.

"No way," said Chief Bell. "You guys have really been cleaning things up in New York."

Eddie and An Li had been friends since grade school when they were ten years old. A playground bully tried to pick on An Li because he was smaller, and Chinese to boot. Eddie, even though they were not real close at the time, took serious exception to the bullying. His temper, which his mother called his "Irish temper", got going, and he was going to jump in the ensuing fight. To Eddie's amazement, An Li jumped into the air and gave the bully a solid kick in the stomach. As the bully bent over, An Li gave him a punch to the nose, and the fight was over. As Eddie liked to say, An Li had the bully crying like a baby. The two had been friends ever since. Eddie learned kung fu from An Li's uncle, and despite the ethnic differences, they became part of each other's family. Eddie's cousin ran a boxing gym, so both boys were proficient boxers. On the streets of New York, each was individually tough. But any of the gangs that foolishly tried to mess with them both found out quickly they were hell on wheels together. An Li had gone on to law school, and was a young but respected lawyer in Chinatown.

When Eddie went back to New York after the big case out West, he had gone to visit An Li. To his shock, An Li informed him that he wanted to become a Secret Service Operative. An Li said he was bored to tears being a lawyer and being cooped up behind a desk all day. Within a week, Chief Taylor had come to New York and sworn An Li in as an operative.

Eddie and some older operatives had taught An Li everything they knew, and the pair was feared and hated by all the known and aspiring counterfeiters in New York.

An Li was a big asset in making the cases suitable for prosecution. He was meticulous with the evidence, and with his lawyer training, his written reports were outstanding. The pair had not had a case go to trial in the two plus years they had worked together. The crooks knew when they were beat, so normally they threw themselves on the mercy of the court and plead out.

"Unfortunately, you fellows are headed out West," said Chief Bell. He took five gold bars out of his desk drawer. "Take a look."

Each operative took a bar and exclaimed, "What the heck!" Each bar had a hollow space in the middle and weighed half of what it should.

"Who in the world would do this?" said An Li, "although, it is a good scheme."

"They flimflammed the wrong man," answered the Chief. "These bars were detected at J.P. Morgan's bank, and he is not happy. They are drilling every bar in their vault. I met Mr. Morgan yesterday in the offices of the good Senator from New York. The Senator is Chairman of the Committee that controls our budget."

"I'm surprised they didn't use the Pinkertons to investigate. Those guys are usually not real careful with legalities," said Eddie.

"The problem is the bars came from the U.S. Assayer's Office in Denver," said the Chief.

"Oh my," said Li. "What about the government's supply of gold bars?"

"The mint in Philadelphia is checking their vault as we speak," answered Bell.

"Don't these things have a mark identifying which company produced them?" asked Eddie.

"They are supposed to, and these had what appeared to be a mark. However, under magnification, it was just a bunch of wiggly lines," informed the Chief. "The good news is the Assayer's Office has narrowed it down to originating from the Cripple Creek Mining District in Colorado. It's also the bad news since there are six outfits that regularly send their gold bars to Denver."

"We'll hustle back to New York and then head for Denver and Cripple Creek," said Eddie.

"Normally that would be fine," said the Chief. "But, in this case, you guys are going to be the only passengers on J.P. Morgan's special train going to Denver. You're going to need western clothes, so just buy them in Denver. And, Mr. Li, please keep the receipts. Your partner seems to always forget. Doris will give you the details regarding your train trip. Oh, Eddie, the Chief sent you this," said Bell flipping a $10 Gold Eagle to Donnally and laughing.

"Oh, Blessed Mother, not this too," complained Eddie as he caught the gold piece in his hand.

"A Deputy U.S. Marshall in Denver took this off a prisoner and thought it felt a little light, so he took it to the Chief. The Chief took it to Joe Walker, and they went to interview the prisoner. With a little encouragement, he identified a fellow named Jeremiah Klein as the source of the coins. Klein supposedly frequents the Wild Horse Saloon in Cripple Creek. He's about 5' 6", long beard and usually wears a slouch miner's hat."

"Great," said Eddie. "Two cases for the price of one!"

The pair left the building and headed to Jonas Beard's boarding house for a good supper.[2]

Early the next morning, An Li and Eddie showed up at the VIP area of Union Station in Washington, D.C. They were met by a slightly older man dressed immaculately. He was standing next to a train consisting of a gleaming engine, a coal car and a long, single car. It was a thing of beauty.

"Mr. Li and Mr. Donnally, I presume," said the man.

"Just Eddie and An Li will be fine," answered An Li.

Figure 4.94   The dining room of Flagler's Number 90, 1898. (Hall of Records)

PHOTO - DINING ROOM

---

[2] **Author's Note:** To learn more about Jonas Beard and Will Scott, see 'Worthy of Trust and Confidence,' a Mouse Gate Series Book, by this author.

"Great. My name is Ralph Cohen, and I am one of Mr. Morgan's assistants. I'll be traveling with you until St. Louis. Besides having business there, Mr. Morgan wants me to educate you on the mining business."

The three climbed aboard the train. As Eddie and An Li looked around, they were astounded.

Ralph Cohen said, "Your reaction is pretty much the same as everyone who sees this car for the first time. Isn't it a beauty?"

"That's an understatement," said Eddie.

There were cut glass chandeliers and polished wooden tables with plush chairs. Two porters appeared and stowed away their small amount of luggage.

"There is one stateroom toward the front and two more in the back," said Cohen. "Let's sit," he said, as they felt the train slowly leaving the station.

A uniformed porter came toward them. "This is Alfred," said Cohen. "He is the official conductor on this train."

Eddie and An Li rose slightly and introduced themselves, shaking hands with Alfred.

"Would you gentlemen care for anything?" asked Alfred.

"We're fine," said Eddie, answering for himself and An Li. "We got breakfast before we left."

"I'm fine too, Alfred, but why don't you bring us some coffee once the train gets up and going?" instructed Cohen.

"Yes sir," said Alfred, heading for the front of the car.

"I'm sure you are curious about Mr. Morgan and Senator Vaughn asking your Chief for help," said Cohen.

"A little," said Eddie. "Most of the big business people go to Pinkerton."

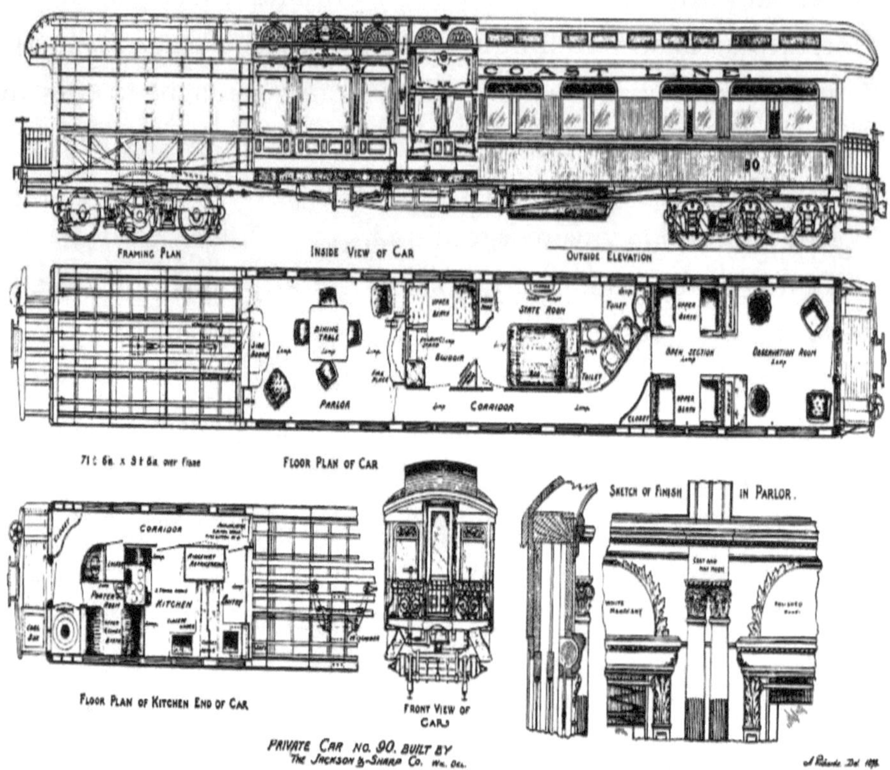

Figure 4.93 Jackson and Sharp produced the Number 90 for Henry M. Flagler, president of the Florida East Coast Railway, in 1898. (Railroad Car Journal, August 1898)

PHOTO - SCHEMATIC OF CAR #90, PRIVATE RAIL CAR BUILT FOR FLORIDA RAILROAD MAGNATE, HENRY FLAGLER, COURTESY OF THE NATIONAL RAILWAY HISTORICAL SOCIETY)

"Ah, Pinkerton," said Cohen. "Mr. Morgan is a forward thinker, and he finds the Pinkertons long on brawn but short on shrewdness. After your Department's success with the case against the former Cabinet members, he holds your agency in high esteem; not to mention that Pinkerton himself likes to brag and see his name in newsprint."

When An Li and Eddie didn't reply, Cohen continued. "I'm going to tell you how people like Mr. Morgan and others conduct mining business. Miners are a strange lot, gentlemen. They will start a shaft with a rich vein, but before long, they need capital for ore cars, hoists and other such things. They try to get someone to lend them the money, but almost everyone shies away from loaning money to small miners. The miners are desperate, so they go to a Gold Mining Exchange in whatever mining district they are in and sign a contract to issue shares of mine stock to raise capital for mining equipment. Based on assay reports, the stock exchange representative and the miner agree on a price for a stock certificate and on how many shares to issue. The miners quite often don't retain that many shares. The stock exchange then sells the stock openly. The buy/sell price fluctuates quite a bit in a boom town like Cripple Creek. The miners don't really care; they are raising the money they need to keep mining. As I said, the stock exchange sells the shares on the open market. Large syndicates headed by businessmen like Mr. Morgan employ bird dogs to "sniff" out promising claims and begin buying up the shares. The miners don't notice or care -- all they want to do is mine and follow the gold vein. Unfortunately for them, if they are on a rich vein, they wake up one day and are met by lawyers and the Sheriff. They discover that somebody else owns most of the share of their mine as they are being escorted off the claim."

Eddie looked at An Li, who said, "It is all legal Eddie, and business is king. Even if the miners have some shares, the syndicates own the rest and are in control."

Eddie and An Li had been so engrossed with Ralph Cohen's story, they never noticed that the train had picked up speed and was moving rapidly through rural areas.

"Here's your coffee, gentlemen," said Alfred, bearing a large silver service.

"I've got some paperwork to take care of," said Cohen. "I'll take mine in the office, Alfred. I'm sure Eddie and An Li want to digest everything I've told them. I hope you have found it helpful. These are some historic chronicles of the Cripple Creek Mining District that I've left for you," he continued, pointing to some paper volumes on the adjacent table. "It is really 'some place', according to these articles."

"Sweet Jesus!" exclaimed Eddie, when Cohen had gone. "No wonder they call these guys robber barons!"

"I agree with you one hundred percent," said An Li. "I said it was legal, not right."

"You remember those counterfeit stock certificates?" asked Eddie, knowing An Li forgot nothing.

"I see where you're going. Maybe we could use a counterfeit stock certificate scam to get in with the crooks, if we can't find Jeremiah Klein," answered An Li.

"When Cohen comes back, we can ask him where real stock certificates are printed," said Eddie.

"What say we read about this 'boom town' in the meantime?" suggested An Li.

It was several hours later when Alfred reappeared. "I've spoken with Mr. Cohen, and if it's okay with you gentlemen, I'll serve lunch in about 30 minutes."

"Sounds good," said Eddie.

After a lunch that rivaled one you could get at any of the fanciest New York restaurants, An Li said, "Ralph, we need you and Mr. Morgan to understand that a case like this can be extremely difficult. We are, for lack of a better term, going in cold. Cripple Creek is filled with all kinds of scams, and we only have one guy to look for. Eddie and I have been discussing various ways to get involved with the criminals doing this, and we have an idea that could help us. Where do these stock certificates that are issued in Cripple Creek at the Gold Exchange come from?"

Ralph Cohen's face broke into a wide grin. "You gentlemen are in luck. Mr. Morgan owns the company that prints the stock certificates.   Actually, the basic stock certificates are all the same. They differ in color, and sometimes people want a special border, but the Gold Exchange I'm sure buys plain Jane certificates. All they do is have someone add the mine name and number of shares using calligraphy. It looks fancy, but they are not really all that different. What do you need?"

"We made a couple of counterfeit stock certificate cases last year, and we think a stock scam might help us get close to these criminals. It's always amazing how crooks will so easily trust another crook," said Eddie. "Do you think we could get some blank stock certificates? An Li is very good at calligraphy."

"No problem," replied Ralph. "When I get off in St. Louis, I'll wire back to see what the Cripple Creek Gold Exchange has bought in the past, and I'll get it to you right away. In fact, given the urgency, I'll get the train to stop in Cincinnati and send the wire. I believe I can get them to Denver before you have to leave."

"That will be great," said Eddie, raising his glass in a toast.

The train got to Cincinnati before dinner, and Cohen got off to send his wire. He got back on rubbing his hands together and smiling. "The instructions are on their way via a courier, and I'm confident the blank certificates will be close behind you in Denver."

"We think that will be a big help," said An Li.

"You two are impressive," complimented Cohen. "Would you have any interest in coming to work for Mr. Morgan when this is over?"

An Li quickly glanced at Eddie and answered diplomatically. "That's very flattering, but we really enjoy what we do, so I don't think so right now."

"Well, if you ever change your mind and are just interested or if the grass looks greener, you let me know," said Cohen, giving them his card. "I know Mr. Morgan has a reputation, but I can assure you he is fair and generous with his staff. I could tell you didn't really care for the mining business, but that's the way it's done. Mr. Morgan has quietly supported improving conditions for the miners and their families. Confrontation with unions and strikes are really bad for business. The animosity between owners and unions can last a long time. We have started to distance ourselves from the Pinkertons because of their strong arm tactics. Anyway, I've got some more work to do, but we can re-convene at dinner."

At dinner, Alfred served another meal suitable for the finest restaurants in New York. Over after-dinner brandies, Eddie remarked, "a man could get used to this life."

Cohen laughed. "Mr. Morgan can be a great friend and boss, but you don't want to be his enemy."

"I can only imagine," said An Li.

"I'll say goodnight gentlemen," said Cohen. "We pass through St. Louis early, so I'll just jump off there. I doubt you will even notice, but you gentlemen just let Alfred know when you want breakfast. It was a pleasure meeting you, and good luck."

After Cohen left, Eddie looked at An Li and said, "You know me too well."

An Li laughed. "I could feel your Irish temper going up."

"You know how many Irish lads have had their heads

busted by those Pinkerton thugs working for the robber barons," fumed Eddie.

"Maybe, just maybe, he's telling the truth about Morgan wanting to avoid conflicts since it's bad for business," said An Li.

"Business and money are king to those guys," said Eddie, "so you may be right, but that would be the only reason."

Once Cohen was gone, they had insisted on Alfred eating with them for the rest of the trip. Alfred had told them stories about some of the people that had been on the Special. Eddie and An Li had Alfred rolling with laughter at some of the case stories from New York. After another day or so, they were pulling into Denver.

"Thanks for taking such good care of us, Alfred," said Eddie as they were disembarking the train.

"It was my pleasure, gentlemen, and good luck," answered Alfred. "You be sure and look me up when you get back. I can't wait to hear the tale."

CHAPTER 4

The couple of weeks before their Thanksgiving Day break seemed to last an eternity for the trio. As it turned out, only Mimi and Abuelo and the three kids made the trip to Orlando.

"You three just go do your thing, but call us every hour or so," instructed Mimi after they got to the park.

"Does anybody care where we go first?" asked Maggie.

"Let's go to the Haunted Mansion cemetery first," said Lizzie, "just in case."

"Okay," said Stephen. "I guess it's as good a place as any to start."

There was nothing in the cemetery, and after going on six other attractions, the trio was discouraged.

"I'm telling you that Ace likes this," groused Stephen. "I bet he's watching us and laughing."

"You better be careful," said Lizzie. "That shillelagh of his looks pretty hard."

"Don't worry, Lizzie," said Maggie. "Nothing is harder than Stephen's head."

"Ha, ha," said Stephen, as they got in line for Thunder Mountain.

They quickly called Mimi to tell her where they were. As it worked out, there was a family of five ahead of the trio, so they ended up in the last car of the ride alone. As they moved into the darkness, all of a sudden, everything was totally quiet. In the darkness, a glowing shape appeared on the plastic dash of their car. It was identical to the shape of the gold coin Lizzie was carrying.

"This is it. This is it!" cried Stephen excitedly.

"Here we go," said Maggie, holding on a little tighter.

"Hurry and put it in, Lizzie," ordered Stephen.

Lizzie dug the gold coin out of her pocket, and slowly pushing it toward the glowing outline, blurted, "I hope we know what we are doing."

The three blinked as they entered the daylight.

"Oh wow!" cried Maggie.

Instead of the plastic car they had been riding in, they found themselves in a 1900 narrow gauge passenger rail car. They were assaulted with the noise of the wheels clicking on the rails and the wind rushing through the open windows.

"Look at our clothes," said Stephen. "I didn't feel a thing."

"Neither did I," said Lizzie.

Stephen was wearing old style blue jeans and a western style shirt with a cowboy hat. The two girls were dressed similarly, with boots, but Maggie had on a vest and neither was wearing cowboy hats.

"Look outside," said Maggie. "We're obviously in the mountains somewhere, probably Colorado. I remember reading about these narrow gauge railroads in one of my history books."

The three started at a series of large booms, which seemed to reverberate around them.

"What was that?" asked Lizzie.

"Sounded like thunder," answered Maggie.

"Yeah, but the sun's out, and I don't see any clouds," added

Stephen.

"Howdy kids," said a train conductor, who appeared suddenly and was standing beside their seats.

"What was all that noise, sir?" asked Lizzie, politely.

The conductor laughed. "Don't you kids know? This is Thunder Canyon. At least that's what everybody calls it. You're riding through some of the richest gold mining areas in the whole State of Colorado. Those booms are from all the blasting going on in the mines."

"Which canyon is it exactly?" asked Maggie.

"Oh, that's just a nickname for this area, Missy," answered the conductor. "Almost all the mountains you see are being mined. Those multiple booms you hear are dynamite blasts from different mines on different mountains. Not to mention, in some of the canyons, you get echoes. I've got to check everyone's tickets, so I might as well start with you three."

All three sucked in their breath as there was another series of loud booms.

"Here you are, sir," said Lizzie, handing over three tickets she had found in her shirt pocket.

"Thanks," said the conductor. "We don't get many kids by themselves on this run, so enjoy the ride."

He moved on, and Stephen and Maggie let out their breath.

"Good work, Lizzie," said Stephen.

"I just felt the tickets in my pocket," said Lizzie. "I have no idea how they got there."

"Let me look at them," said Maggie. "It says round trip tickets from Leadville to Cripple Creek, Denver and Rio Grande Railroad, issued 11/21/1900."

"At least we know the date," said Stephen.

"Hold on," Maggie said, feeling in her vest pocket. She

pulled out a note and read it aloud, "Uncle Eddie, Eldridge Hotel, Room 314."

They were bombarded with another round of booms that seemed to be right beside the train.

"I'll be glad to get off this thing," said Stephen. "Those blasts feel like they could just blow us right off the tracks."

Within the hour, they noticed the train was entering a town that looked so busy it seemed to be growing before their eyes.

"I guess this is what they call a boom town," said Maggie.

"Here, kids," said the conductor, handing them each a traveling bag from an overhead rack.

"Thanks, sir," said Lizzie.

"You wouldn't happen to know the Eldridge Hotel, would you?" asked Stephen.

"That's an easy one," laughed the conductor. "When you come out of the station, just look straight ahead. You'll see the Eldridge up the hill at the end of the street. Can't miss it."

"Thanks," said Maggie. "Are you getting off here?"

"I wish," said the conductor. "Unfortunately, we unhook this set of cars and leave them here and pick up the ones we brought up yesterday. The freight people unload all the shipped items after we pull out."

"You go back empty?" asked Lizzie.

"Oh no," said the conductor. "We have a fair number of passengers, but not so much freight. Sometimes we have a Wells Fargo car carrying gold."

The trio stepped off the train onto the platform and headed for the station building. The sign on the side of the building identified it as the Midland Terminal. The lobby of the building was crowded with people presumably headed back to Leadville.

As they exited outside and started up the wooden sidewalk, Stephen exclaimed, "Jeez, what is that smell?"

"What did you expect?" asked Maggie. "There's a ton of horses, not to mention outhouses!"

"I never thought about that," said Lizzie, wrinkling her nose.

"Hopefully, it will be better up the hill at the hotel," said Stephen, picking up the pace.

When the trio entered, the hotel desk clerk eyed them suspiciously. "What do you kids want? We don't do handouts."

"We're here to meet our Uncle Eddie in room 314," said Lizzie, jumping in politely before Stephen and Maggie could tell the clerk off.

"Well, go ahead then," sniffed the desk clerk, slightly less pompous.

When they got to room 314, Lizzie tentatively knocked on the door. It opened abruptly, and there stood Eddie Donnally in the flesh. All three knew Eddie from their first trip through the Gate, but this was different.

"Hello, Uncle Eddie," said Lizzie. "Ace sent us to help you."

CHAPTER 5

Eddie Donnally didn't think he could be more surprised. He stared at the three kids. "Sweet Jesus," he exclaimed. "You're kids!"

"That would be us," said Maggie, leading the trio into the room.

"Let me get this straight. My supposedly guardian leprechaun sent me kids," he muttered.

An Li, sitting in a side chair, said, "not him again, Eddie."

"Yeah, he showed up just as I was going to the train station to go to Washington. I thought I saw him on a street corner and he saluted me with his shillelagh. I didn't tell you since I was hoping it didn't mean anything. I should have known better," he explained.

"Hello sir. My name is Lizzie," she said, doing her usual and turning toward An Li.

"I'm An Li," he replied. "I'm Eddie's partner."

Maggie and Stephen quickly introduced themselves.

"We are . . ." Maggie realized she was going to explain where they were from, but the words wouldn't come out.

"You won't be able to tell us where you are from," said Eddie. "It's some kind of leprechaun spell."

"You can use whatever skills and knowledge you possess, but you can't talk about certain things. It will be just like that-- you will start to say something and then the words won't come out," continued An Li.

"You know Ace too, Mr. Li?" asked Stephen.

"To know him is to love him," laughed Li.

"First thing I've got to do is get another room for you girls," said Eddie. "You can bunk with me, Stephen. I'll be right back."

"Did Ace give you any specific information?" asked An Li.

"Not really," answered Maggie. "He just said Eddie and his partner needed a wee bit of help."

"I'll bring you up-to-date," said Li, showing them a gold bar.

"It's got a hole in it," said Maggie.

"That's exactly what we are here about," said Li. "Someone is making counterfeit gold bars and shipping them out to banks."

"Do you have any leads?" asked Stephen.

"Nothing except they are from around here," answered Li. "In addition," said Li, flipping the counterfeit $10 gold piece to Stephen, "we've got this to deal with. We suspect the people counterfeiting the bars are using the gold to make these coins."

"Cool," said Stephen. "I've only seen these . . ." He was going to say, "in history books," but the words wouldn't come out. "I've never seen one before," he finally managed to get out.

"I'm assuming it's counterfeit too," stated Maggie.

"Yes," said Li. "We know it came from Cripple Creek, and a man named Jeremiah Klein."

"What's your plan?" asked Lizzie, trying to sound like a TV investigator.

Before Li could answer, Eddie came back with a room key.

"You girls are across the hall," said Eddie.

"Why don't you tell them our plan?" asked An Li laughing.

"We don't have much of one," grumbled Eddie.

"Surely you must have something in mind," said Maggie.

"First, said An Li, "we will split up and reconnoiter the town.

This place is really booming. We are going to start at the Wild Horse Saloon. Klein supposedly hangs out at the Wild Horse and we're hoping to find him and put the squeeze on."

"We can help with that," said Stephen. "Nobody notices kids hanging around."

"Ace didn't say anything to you at all?" asked Eddie.

"No," said Maggie. "Like we told An Li, he just said Eddie Donnally and his partner are going to need a wee bit of help."

An Li spoke up. "Here is a map of the town. Let's see what we can sort out."

"You three can't go into any gambling saloons or bordellos," said Eddie, jumping in.

"We can hang outside and see who comes and goes and stuff," said Stephen.

"Kid, you talk funny," said An Li. "Anybody ever tell you that?"

Before Stephen could answer, Eddie said laughingly, "An Li will be disguised as a Chinaman!"

"Ignore him," said An Li. "What he means is that I will be dressed as a Chinese worke

"You guys know how to do that?" asked Lizzie incredulously.

"Yeah, no problem," said Eddie. "I have a cousin who works in New York in the theater doing make-up. She gave us a crash course and everything we need. This won't be the first time we've had to resort to disguises. Once, An Li disguised himself as an old woman."

"Here," growled An Li. "Ignore him. You kids take this map and just get familiar with the town. It's not totally accurate. Cripple Creek is growing too fast."

"I'll meet you in the hotel restaurant at 6 o'clock sharp," said

Eddie. "Stay together and be careful."

"Yes sir," answered Lizzie.

"You can just leave your bags here," said Eddie.

The kids stood up and scooted out the door.

After the kids left, Eddie and An Li stared at each other. "I'd strangle that little leprechaun if I could get my hands on him," barked Eddie. "I wonder if you could be charged with murder if you kill a leprechaun!"

"We never covered that topic in law school," laughed An Li. "We might as well make the best of it, though. Nobody pays much attention to kids, like he said."

"I guess," answered Eddie.

"Anyway," said An Li, "I'll change and start, what did that kid say, hanging with some of the Chinese. They notice us even less than they do kids."

"Okay, I'll see you tonight or tomorrow morning," said Eddie, as An Li left the room.

"Ace, what the heck are you doing?" muttered Eddie to no one in particular.

CHAPTER 6

The kids blew past the front desk clerk without notice. Outside, they found a bench and sat down to look at the map.

"The smell is not much better up here," said Lizzie.

"You'll get used to it," said Stephen, feeling in his pants pocket. "Hey, I've got some money!"

They all stared at the shiny gold coins and the other two quickly emptied their pockets.

"Hey, we've got some money, too!" exclaimed the girls.

"These things would be worth a lot of money back home," said Stephen.

"Wow," said Maggie. "You were able to talk about home. I guess that crazy leprechaun spell only applies when we try to talk to someone else."

"Let's walk around and see what we can see," said Stephen. "I think we ought to stay together until we check out the town."

"We're sticking together, period," said Maggie, grabbing hold of Lizzie's hand.

By late in the afternoon, the trio had been up and down every significant street at least once. They didn't bother with the many side streets. Each main street was serviced by a trolley car. The dynamite booms were not noticeable, except for a few times, and they seemed far away.

"We better beat it back to the hotel," said Maggie, pointing to the courthouse clock. "It's 5:45 already."

"Yeah, and I'm starving," said Stephen.

"You're always starving," said Lizzie.

"I wonder what they have to eat in 1900. Somehow, I don't think it will be pizza," muttered Stephen.

As they entered the hotel restaurant, a man over in the corner motioned. When they got closer, all three stopped and stared.

"Top of the morning," said Eddie. He was wearing a full but neat beard, and was wearing a pair of spectacles.

"Jeez," said Stephen. "We barely recognized you."

"That's the whole point, laddie," laughed Eddie.

"You know, sometimes you sound a lot like Ace," said Lizzie.

"That is not a compliment," Eddie barked. "But it's okay," softening his tone due to the stricken look on Lizzie's face. "What did you think of Cripple Creek?" asked Eddie, changing the subject.

"It smells," replied Lizzie, wrinkling her nose.

The other three laughed.

"Okay, besides the smell, what did you think?" asked Eddie.

"It was interesting," said Maggie. "There were so many different looking people. Some wore fancy clothes and dresses, while others were covered in dirt."

"There are saloons everywhere," said Stephen.

"Nobody paid any attention to us, even though there are not a lot of kids hanging around," answered Maggie.

A waitress came over and gave the kids menus.

"What's good here, Uncle Eddie?" asked Lizzie.

"The steak is pretty good, and Colorado mutton is pretty good in a stew," said Eddie.

The kids looked at each other, and Maggie said, "We will all have the steak and baked potatoes, please."

The waitress nodded to Eddie and headed for the kitchen.

"She didn't ask us how we wanted our steak," said Stephen.

Eddie laughed. "This ain't New York City kid. Out here you pretty much get it however they serve it."

"After supper, I'm going to go to the saloon, do a little gambling and looking around. Li is down in the Chinese quarter nosing about," informed Eddie.

"You three are only going to work during the day right now. Some of these gambling places and saloons get kinda rough at night. Li and I probably wouldn't be in a position to help you if you got into trouble."

"We're all pretty tired," said Maggie. I'm assuming things get going early around here."

"Yeah, they do," said Eddie. "There are some magazines and newspapers up in the room if you want to read."

The group didn't do a lot more talking since several people sat down at adjacent tables within earshot. They all got apple pie for dessert, and afterwards, Eddie headed out to the saloon and the kids trooped upstairs.

Once in the room, Stephen said, "Look at this, Field and Stream magazine. Abuello gets this at home. Look at the size of the elk on the cover. I heard from Colter Turner that elk tastes great. He and his dad always come hunting out here."

"These newspapers are funny," said Lizzie. "They report every little thing. Mrs. Johnson reports the theft of one chicken from the coop in her backyard," read Lizzie, laughing.

"I'm tired guys. You read all you want, but I'm going to bed," replied Maggie, as she headed across the hall.

CHAPTER 7

Eddie strolled into the Wild Horse and made his way to the bar. It was a typical western bar, smoky and loud. There were a couple of blackjack tables, a roulette wheel, a faro table and a poker table. The bar was along the right-hand wall, and there was so much business, two bartenders were at work. The place was lit by electric chandeliers and was pretty bright for a saloon. Miners are a strange breed thought Eddie. They work really hard and then give away whatever they make to saloons and gambling houses.

"What's your poison, mister?" asked the barkeep.

"I'll take a whisky," said Eddie, adopting an Irish accent, "preferably one from the old country."

"It will cost you a little more, but I happen to have a nice bottle," answered the bartender.

Eddie paid for his drink and casually looked around the large saloon. He carefully studied the games of chance. One of An Li's uncles in New York was a gambling expert and had taught Eddie and An Li every trick in the book.

"Hello stranger," said a man in a black frock coat with a bright vest.

"Hello yourself," said Eddie. "My name is Eddie Donnally."

"I'm J.T. Raines. I own this den of inequity," said the man laughing.

Raines was about six feet tall with slick-backed black hair.

He had a slight paunch and was obviously used to the good life.

"Any place that has whisky from the old country is my kind of place. You seem to have a thriving business," remarked Eddie.

"Yes, it's turned out quite well," said Raines. "What's your line? You don't look like a miner?"

"No," said Eddie, looking around. "There's no money in that. I represent several syndicates in New York and specialize in buying claims that can't be worked by individual miners. Here's my card. We pay a handsome finder's fee. You would appear to be in a position to know the lay of the land around here."

"You've come to the right place," exclaimed Raines. "I have a couple of men who keep their eye on which miners are doing well and which are not. I'm very careful who I extend credit to."

"I was afraid this would not be a fruitful place. The dynamiting seems to be non-stop. Usually that means some of the big boys are already here and have things sewn up," said Eddie.

"Oh no," said Raines. "Every hard pan miner around here seems to have dynamite. A lot of them were in the Spanish War and have a little experience with dynamite. They just dig a hole, fill it with dynamite and blow it up. Then they pick through the rubble and bring the gold ore to the assayer, hoping to have found a vein outcropping. Around here they call them glory holes. You see them all over the place."

"You don't take gold here?" asked Eddie.

"No," said Raines. "The smelter pays them gold eagles or paper money. Most of them prefer the gold coins. They all have the gold fever."

"That's good to know. Thanks," said Eddie. "In the past, the syndicate has set up its own smelter, but if you have a reliable one here, it would be perfect."

"The owner is a good friend. If you come around tomorrow around 11:00 a.m., I'll introduce you," replied Raines.

"Sounds good," said Eddie. "I'll be here."

"Well, I better circulate a little and keep an eye on things," said Raines, moving away from Eddie.

Eddie again focused on the games of chance. They were very good, but every game was crooked. Eddie had another glass of Irish whisky and then headed to the hotel. He looked hard, but didn't see anyone he thought could be Jeremiah Klein.

Powell and Braxton entered the Wild Horse after Eddie was gone.

"Howdy boss," said Powell, sidling up beside Raines.

"Where the heck have you two been? Is everything alright at the mine?" snapped Raines.

"They were working hard boss. And take a look at their latest," said Powell, reaching into his vest pocket.

"Not here you fool," barked Raines. "Meet me in the office."

A few minutes later, the trio were looking at a bright 1896S Coronet Gold Eagle $10 gold piece.

"Outstanding," said Raines. "The ridges on the outside are not real sharp, but the weight and look is almost perfect."

"They said they would have another batch ready in two or three days," said Powell.

"As usual, I'm sending this batch to my brother in Victor. But you guys are the only ones making the delivery. After the Klein mess, I don't trust anybody else," ordered Raines.

"We're headed to the all-night cafe boss," said Powell. "Send for us if there are any problems. We won't be gone too long."

Raines left his office to greet more of his patrons, and the two hungry thugs moved away.

PHOTO - THE $10 GOLD PIECE WAS KNOWN AS AN EAGLE, THE $20 GOLD PIECE WAS CALLED A DOUBLE EAGLE, THE $5 GOLD PIECE WAS CALLED A HALF EAGLE, AND THE $2.50 GOLD PIECE WAS THE QUARTER EAGLE.

CHAPTER 8

Stephen woke with a start at the sound of the Molly McGee's steam whistle at 6:00 a.m. It also woke Eddie up.

"Top of the morning, lad," said Eddie cheerfully.

"You're not kidding," said Stephen, not much of a morning person. "How did it go last night?" He had been fast asleep when Eddie came back.

"The Wild Horse runs nothing but crooked games, but I did meet the owner," answered Eddie.

"Why don't the police or somebody do something about the crooked games?" asked Stephen.

Eddie laughed. "You're kidding, right? The town marshal is probably getting paid by the saloon owners. He only comes around if there's trouble, but most of those guys have their own thugs anyway."

"So last night was a bust?" asked Stephen.

"Not entirely," answered Eddie. "The owner, J.T. Raines, is going to introduce me to the owner of a gold ore crusher and smelter. This kind of operation needs a smelter. That's where they make the bars. Unfortunately, there was no sign of Jeremiah Klein at the Wild Horse."

There was a slight tap at the door. Stephen opened it to the two girls.

"Morning, Uncle Eddie," beamed Lizzie, a morning person.

"Top of the morning, ladies," answered Eddie.

"Is there a ladies room somewhere?" asked Maggie.

"You're in luck. This is the best hotel in town, and they have indoor plumbing. Down the hall to your left, just turn the sign around if it says gents," answered Eddie.

Maggie rolled her eyes as she and Lizzie headed for the "ladies room".

In just a minute or two, there were three soft taps on the door. "Let An Li in kid," said Eddie.

Normally, Stephen would have bristled at someone calling him kid, but with Eddie, it wasn't like that. It was more like a nickname. He kind of liked it. Stephen opened the door and his mouth dropped open. In front of him was a Chinese man with round glasses, a Fu Manchu mustache, a round Chinese hat, and a long pig tail. He straightened up and said "Good Morning." Stephen quickly shut the door.

"I would have never known it was you," gasped Stephen.

"Exactly," answered a laughing An Li and Eddie in unison.

Just then, the girls tapped on the door and walked in. Like Stephen, both were shocked.

"You look amazing," sputtered Maggie.

"Thank you, I think," answered An Li.

"Let's get down to business," suggested Eddie. "I'm starving, and unfortunately, dressed as he is, they won't serve An Li in the dining room." He briefly summarized his previous night's activities for An Li and the girls, finishing with the fact that there was no sign of Jeremiah Klein.

"I can verify that according to the Chinese community, all the games in town are bent. The Chinese people here either worked on the railroad or are their descendants. There are no triads or criminal groups like in New York. They all seem to be honest, hardworking people. None of them are miners. There are some laundries, boarding and bath houses and a big saw mill owned by several Chinese men that is interesting, as well as a general store. The store sells things to the Chinese and to a lot of the local people, as well as the miners. The store has been here a long time, and the big mining companies never bothered with building a company store or company houses. It's just on the edge of Chinatown."

"We may have lucked out. There is also an old man who is an acupuncturist and an herbalist that is from the same village as my grandfather. You kids can send a telegram to New York and see if my grandfather knows this man or his family. If he does, then I believe we should enlist his help," continued An Li.

"That would save us a lot of time and keep anyone from noticing us," answered Eddie.

"Yeah, I can only ask so many questions without people starting to notice and acting suspicious," said An Li.

"That's no problem, but," looking at the other two, "we're not real familiar with the telegraph," answered Mags.

Now it was Eddie and An Li's turn to be speechless. Recovering himself, Eddie said, "it is easy really. An Li will write out what he wants sent and where. You just give the Western Union guy money and he will send it."

"We'll just sign it, your nephew, Stephen," said An Li. "Grandfather will know it's from me. There is a Western Union Office close to his shop in New York, so he should get it and answer back real quick. You can just hang around in the area and keep checking back with the operator."

"Where will we find you?" asked Maggie.

"I'm going with the owner of the Wild Horse at 11:00. I'll be out of touch for a couple of hours. If something significant happens, just come back to the hotel and we can meet at 6:00

p.m. for dinner," answered Eddie. "You three can go downstairs and get breakfast. Just tell Jamie, the waitress, to charge it to my room," said Eddie. "Then hustle over to the Western Union. Here's some money. You can go into the dry goods store near there and get some more clothes. Your bags were kinda light," instructed Eddie.

"Here's the message," said An Li.

Stephen folded it and put it in his vest pocket.

"Okay," Maggie answered, and they all hustled downstairs.

"So, what do you think, An Li?" asked Eddie.

"If my grandfather knows the pharmacist's family, we are really in luck. He can gather a lot of information for us. You know how it is; most people don't notice the workers, especially the Chinese workers. A lot of them believe the Chinese don't understand English," answered An Li.

"Thank goodness for ignorant people," replied Eddie. "Meeting this crusher and smelter guy might be good, because you really need someone on the inside to get the gold bars, unless the crooks have set up a small smelter and are making a few bars at a time and then substituting. But that would be extremely difficult, if not, impossible to do in large quantities."

"That's one reason I'm anxious to get information from the saw mill guy. Everyone around here needs wood, and if he's making any unusual deliveries, it might identify a sight," reflected An Li aloud.

"I'll say a couple of Hail Mary's that your grandfather will know this guy," laughed Eddie

"What about the kids?" asked An Li.

"I don't know," said Eddie. "I guess we need to keep them close. I have no idea why they are here, but Ace has never really let us down."

"Agreed - aggravated us, but not let us down," laughed An Li. "I'll come back tonight and we can see what's what."

"Go with God, my son," said Eddie, making the sign of the cross.

"With pleasure," said An Li going out the door.

CHAPTER 9

"Wow, mom would have a hissy fit if she knew we were eating like this," said Lizzie. They each had eggs, bacon and biscuits with gravy.

"Yeah, there's no such thing as light around here," said Maggie.

"It's a good thing we like coffee a little too. There's not many other choices," added Stephen.

"This milk is really thick. It tastes good, though." said Lizzie.

"And my mom would call this a heart attack on a plate," said Maggie, digging in and laughing.

After breakfast, they trooped over to the Western Union and sent their message. While the girls were in the dry goods store, Stephen sat outside on a bench fascinated by all the activity. There was a stagecoach that said Wells Fargo, and looked just like the pictures of the one at the bank at home. He stared at a heavy freight wagon with an eight-horse team. All types of buggies were going up and down the street. There were one-horse rigs and then, occasionally, a fancy carriage with what looked like a matched pair of horses. He saw what he guessed were miners leading burros laden with picks and shovels. This looks like one of those shows Abuelo likes to watch on History TV, thought Stephen. None of the history books or shows talk about the smell and the noise, though. He could hear a piano playing faintly from someplace. Just then, two guys came out of the hardware store behind him carrying several boxes of ammunition. They took no notice of Stephen as the one man stopped to roll a cigarette.

"That was a nice bonus the boss gave us for taking care of that Klein fella," said the one.

"Yeah, did you see the look on his face as he went off the train?" laughed the other.

The two men walked off, but Stephen had heard every word. For a moment, he debated on whether to go or stay. He looked for Maggie and Lizzie, but when he didn't see them, decided to take a chance and follow the two men.

Actually, Stephen thought after a few blocks, this surveillance stuff was not too bad. The men were in no hurry, and he was able to hang back and even crossed over to the other side of the street like he had seen in a movie. Ultimately, the two went to the Wild Horse Saloon and knocked on the closed front door. The saloon had a gaudy paint job and there was a large rearing horse on top of the front sign. Stephen couldn't see who opened the door, but the men were let right in, even though the place was obviously closed. "Bingo," Stephen thought, and immediately headed back the way he came.

Although he had only been gone around thirty minutes, the girls were frantically pacing the wooden sidewalk.

"Where have you been?" cried Maggie, with her hands on her hips and fear in her voice.

"Easy," answered Stephen. "You look like Aunt Sandy when she's on the war path!"

"This better be good," chimed Lizzie, seeing her chance to jump in.

"You won't believe it," said Stephen excitedly. "These two men came out of the store and one was carrying a couple of boxes of ammunition. The other started rolling a cigarette, and they were joking about a guy named Klein. They said their boss gave them a bonus, and I'm telling you, it sounded like they threw this guy Klein off the train!"

"No way!" said Lizzie.

"Yes, way," said Stephen. "I tailed them until they went into the Wild Horse Saloon. It was closed, but they were let right in."

"You tailed them!" exclaimed Maggie, arching her eyebrows.

"Come on, Mags. Give me a break," pleaded Stephen.

"You're right," she replied. "You did good," she continued, giving him a knuckle bump.

"I'm starving," said Lizzie. "All this pacing and worrying has made me hungry."

"Okay," said Maggie. "There's a cafe across the street that looks half-way respectable."

As the kids sat down, a waitress hurried over. "Hello kids. What will you have? The special today is meat loaf and mashed potatoes."

"We'll have the special," they all answered almost in unison.

"Could we look at the menu, please?" asked Lizzie, "We just want to see what you have for next time."

"Sure, honey," answered the waitress, handing them a menu.

"Look!" exclaimed Stephen, "Boiled tongue in chili sauce, ugh!"

Maggie shivered and read, "Baked pickerel in wine sauce, yuck!"

"Pretty fancy for a cafe," declared Lizzie.

After lunch, the trio trooped back to the Western Union office. There were no customers, but the telegraph operator was writing down an incoming message. When he looked up, he said, "You three are lucky. That was your reply I was taking down. Here it is."

Maggie took the message, and they all sat on the bench in front of the Western Union Office.

"What does it say?" asked Lizzie.

"Here, we can look at it together," Mags answered.

> **REPLY - to NY inquiry. STOP**
> **---Know family well. STOP**
> **Friend with youngest son. STOP**
> **Name Li Chung. STOP**
> **Grandfather**

"Cool," said Stephen. "Let's go find Eddie and An Li."

PHOTO - THIS IS A MORSE-VAIL TELEGRAPH KEY. MESSAGES WERE SENT VIA TELEGRAPH WIRE USING MORSE CODE. MORSE USES A SERIES OF DOTS AND DASHES OR SHORT AND LONG TAPS TO COMMUNICATE BETWEEN TELEGRAPH OPERATORS. THE INTERNATIONALLY RECOGNIZED EMERGENCY SIGNAL SOS, 3 DOTS - 3 DASHES - 3 DOTS, IS MORSE CODE.

"Us being seen with An Li is probably not a good thing, and Eddie is out with that saloon owner. Let's stick to the plan and meet Eddie in the hotel dining room at 6:00 p.m.," said Maggie.

"Great," said Lizzie. "Let's wander around and see what we can see."

"Fine," said Stephen, "but it sure does smell here. No history teacher ever mentioned that!"

"Will you stop?" said Maggie.

The trio was already seated in the hotel dining room when Eddie strolled in at 6:00p.m. He tipped his hat to the waitress and covered her hand with his hands and murmured a few words. She answered with a big smile and waved at the trio.

"Uncle Eddie reminds me of those guys in the soap operas," said Lizzie.

"He's pretty slick with the ladies," admitted Maggie, grudgingly.

"Well, well," said Eddie. "The whole family together again," giving them a broad smile.

"Wait until you hear what we've been doing, Eddie!" exclaimed Stephen, refusing to call Eddie uncle.

"Do tell," replied Eddie, leaning in close.

"Here is the telegram from An Li's grandfather, and it's good news," said Maggie handing over the message.

Eddie scanned the telegram. "Excellent," he said.

"I got real lucky too," blurted Stephen. He quickly outlined his tailing of the two men from the hardware store.

Eddie smiled and scowled at the same time, if such a thing was possible. "You did good kid, but none of you should forget that these are dangerous people. They've already probably killed one man. I don't think we'll be putting the squeeze on Jeremiah Klein."

The kids' enthusiasm quickly died at the seriousness of Eddie's voice.

"We'll pass this info to An Li later, and he can make contact with the Chinese herbalist," said Eddie. "You kids order anything you want -- you've earned it!"

After the waitress took their orders, Eddie turned and asked Stephen to describe the two men he saw.

"One was pretty tall. I guess probably over six feet. He had dark hair and he seemed to have a Northern accent, although I didn't hear them talk much. His clothes looked pretty much like everyone else around here. He had on a brown vest and I could see the end of a holster sticking out under the vest. The other guy was shorter, maybe 5'8" or so, just a little taller than me. He had on one of those long coats you see a lot of people wearing. I'm pretty sure he was carrying a gun too. He had dark hair and was wearing the same kind of hat as the other one. He's the one I heard talking about their bonus," said Stephen. "Oh, and they both had mustaches."

"Excellent," replied Eddie. "We'll pass all this to An Li."

"Here's your dinner, folks," said the waitress, setting down plates in front of everyone.

"Looks great," said Eddie, giving her a big smile.

CHAPTER 10

It was dark by nine o'clock, and An Li showed up shortly after. The kids were playing cards and Eddie was reading the newspaper. Stephen jumped up and opened the door at the slight knock.

"Evening everyone," said An Li.

"Evening yourself," answered Eddie. "You three go ahead before you bust at the seams."

"First," said Maggie, assuming an in-charge air. "Here is the telegram we got back from your grandfather."

An Li quickly scanned the telegram and broke into a big smile. "Most excellent," he exclaimed. "I'll approach the old man first thing tomorrow."

"I've got news too," Stephen blurted. He repeated what he had previously told Eddie.

"I'm glad you three are with us," said An Li.

"Me, too," said Eddie. "The saloon owner introduced me to the manager of the crusher/smelter and the government assayer. Nobody said anything, but I think they were sizing me up. That's what concerns me. They don't know about you kids, but sooner or later they might."

The trio gave Eddie "the evil eye" while An Li shifted his weight back and forth. They suspected something.

"Don't worry. You are going to still be involved," laughed Eddie. "The old Chief's wife has a niece, Mary Helen

McDougal, who runs a boarding house for respectable ladies here in Cripple Creek. She's some kind of do-gooder, so the Chief says. We'll look her up tomorrow and get you three a place to stay."

"But . . . ," started Maggie.

"Don't worry," said Eddie, holding up his hand. "You do good work and we want you to keep doing it."

"That's right," said An Li. You guys have done a helluva job so far."

"We'll get together every day so we will all know what's happening," said Eddie.

"Okay," said Maggie. "But don't forget, Ace said we are here to help you, and here we intend to stay."

"Deal," said Eddie. "You guys go play cards across the hall and let me and An Li talk."

After the kids left, An Li eyed Eddie. "I'm not sure we should leave them out of things."

"I don't plan to," said Eddie. "We've had an amazing day, but you and I both know this is not going to be an easy case. It always worries me when things go this easy in the beginning."

"You're right," said An Li. "We don't want those kids to be a way to get an advantage over us. Not having Klein to put the squeeze on really hurts."

"You wouldn't like to take them over to this Mary Helen?" asked Eddie slyly.

"Not me," said An Li. "She's probably a big old spinster that hates all men, especially a smart-mouthed Irishman. Even money says she's shaped like a potato."

"Beat it," barked Eddie. "I need a good night's sleep before I butt heads with the spinster."

An Li bowed and then went out the door laughing.

At breakfast the next morning, Eddie was his jovial self, while the kids were a little apprehensive.

"Does this lady know anything about you?" asked Maggie.

"I don't know for sure," answered Eddie. "She's close to the Chief's wife, so she probably knows a little at least."

"She's not going to try to send us to some one-room schoolhouse, is she?" grumbled Stephen.

"No. I'm planning on you guys keeping your eyes and ears open and just, as you say, 'hanging'," said Eddie. "I didn't ask you what you thought about the town."

"It was cool," said Stephen. "We saw the Grand Opera House. . ."

"Whoa," said Eddie. "You need to stay off Meyers Avenue, especially late in the day. That's where all the, uh, houses of ill repute are!"

"Yeah, it did seem awfully quiet there during the day compared to other streets," said Maggie.

"You should use the street cars whenever you can. I'd like you to stay close to the Wild Horse and near the telegraph office. We really got lucky learning for sure about the Wild Horse. It was good to get that verified, even if Klein is nowhere to be found. There are well over 100 saloons in town," stated Eddie.

"We'll be careful, Uncle Eddie," said Lizzie. "Don't worry. We're used to big cities."

The other two rolled their eyes as Eddie pushed back from the table and said, "Well, let's go see this Mary Helen."

CHAPTER 11

The Lohmuller claim was at the end of a short draw up a winding, narrow trail. There was one way in and one way out. The mine entrance was just a hole in the wall that went back about five-hundred feet. The claim had never amounted to much and Kira Cassidy had no trouble buying the abandoned claim. As soon as she bought it, she put her three brothers to work enlarging the cabin, which was actually in pretty good shape. The place had a strong well, and in a month, she had the place just like she wanted. There was an out building behind the main cabin that held a small melting furnace. In a room off the main mine tunnel, she had set up a drilling apparatus that her Uncle Tom had made, along with the dies he and Kira had made for the $10 Coronet Eagles.

Kira's dad had been a miner in Cripple Creek, and she had grown up there until she was sixteen when her dad was killed in a mining accident. Allen, Thomas and Nathan had been 12, 10 and 8 years old at the time. Their mother, a bit of a rounder, had immediately shipped the kids back East to Uncle Tom in New York City. She had then gone to Meyers Avenue and began getting paid for doing something she enjoyed anyway.

Uncle Tom and Aunt Meg had no children of their own, so the kids were very welcome. Tom Cassidy was a smart, talented man when it came to making anything. Unfortunately, he belonged to an Irish gang, and due to his skill with equipment, specialized in making counterfeit money -- specifically, counterfeit gold coins. Another uncle, Lloyd, was a skilled plate engraver, and Cousin Forrest was a skilled printer. They had quite the family business going. Kira loved Uncle Tom more than she had her own father, and loved watching him make the shiny gold coins. Paper money just didn't have the same feel or fascination for her. Unfortunately, Aunt Meg had died from TB, and Uncle Tom and Cousin Forrest were currently serving eight-year sentences in Federal Prison, thanks primarily to Eddie Donnally. Kira, now in her mid-20's, had taken her three brothers and returned to Cripple Creek. Along with her, she brought all of Uncle Tom's dies, molds and equipment. He had taught her everything he knew, so she was at least as skilled as he was. In fact, she had a delicate woman's touch with the die press and produced some outstanding counterfeit coins. When they had lived in Cripple Creek before, the boom was just starting. Now, it was a city of 50,000 people, and the money was flowing. As soon as they had hit town and bought the claim, Kira started prowling the saloons and gambling halls hoping to find an outlet for her counterfeit. Many women would have trouble, but not Kira. While her brothers were fairly short and thin, Kira was a big-boned woman who could clearly take care of herself. She wasn't fat, just square built, like a block.

As luck would have it, when she went into the Wild Horse Saloon, she spied J.T. Raines. They had been in school together when they were younger. Her mother hadn't much cared, but her Dad had insisted on all the kids going to school.

"Hello J.T.," said Kira.

"Good Lord, Kira Glynn!" exclaimed J.T.

"It's Kira Cassidy now," she said.

"Jeez. What? It's been ten years since we used to beat up those kids for their milk money," he said laughing.

"Looks like you've been doing pretty good for yourself!" Kira exclaimed, looking around.

"Yeah, there are some easy pickings around here now," said J.T., giving her a wink.

"I've got a proposition for you that I think you'll like," answered Kira.

"Step into my office. I'm sure I'll like what you're offering," he answered.

It had been the beginning of a grand partnership. Together they had developed a scheme for passing the counterfeit gold coins that was working perfectly. Kira's work was excellent, and the coins would easily pass muster with any of the counterfeit detectors used in town.

One night over drinks, Kira had laughingly related how her uncle had taught her how to drill tiny holes in gold coins and then fill the holes in with slivers of metal to bring the coins up to nearly the exact correct weight. The small holes were easily covered with gold, and she had made a small fortune on her own. But the work was time-consuming and Uncle Tom had only used it to train Kira. He then taught her how to engrave and build equipment to make decent quantities of high quality gold coins from scratch that were nearly undetectable. Tom had marveled at Kira's ability. She was a natural.

J.T.'s brother owned a saloon and gambling hall in Victor, and he only paid out in counterfeit coins struck by Kira. It was a perfect setup. The counterfeit was paid out away from the Wild Horse. Passing counterfeit outside of your own neighborhood was one of Tom Cassidy's first rules.

PHOTO - COUNTERFEIT COIN DETECTOR - THIS DETECTOR WAS USED FOR GOLD AND SILVER COINS. IN ADDITION TO MODERN DENOMINATIONS, IT CHECKED $2.50 AND $3.00 COINS. IT ALSO HAS A SLOT TO CHECK 1/2 OZ, 1 OZ, 1 1/2 OZ AND 2 OZ GOLD BARS. THESE SMALL GOLD BARS WERE SOMETIMES USED IN THE GOLD FIELDS AS CURRENCY.

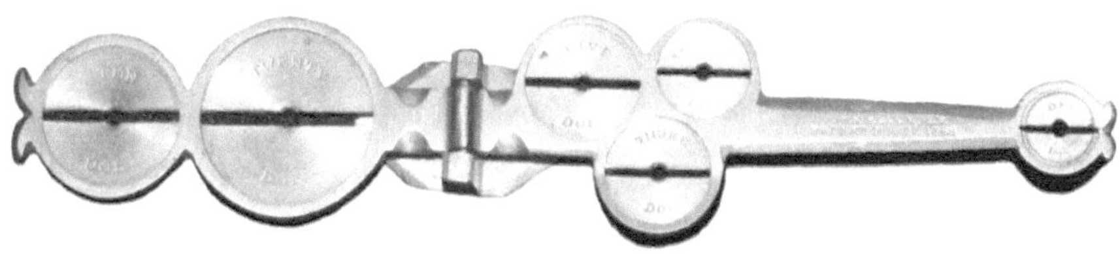

PHOTO - COUNTERFEIT COIN DETECTOR 1880'S - THIS IS A BALANCE SCALE THAT WAS USED TO CHECK ONE DOLLAR, 1 1/2 DOLLAR, 10 DOLLAR AND 20 DOLLAR GOLD COINS. YOU COULD CHECK WEIGHT AND WIDTH.

After several successful months, Kira stopped by the Wild Horse to drop off coins.

"You know, Kira, I have an idea," said J.T. "Gold bars are very common around here. All we'd have to do is get our hands on some and maybe you could drill them out like you did with the coins in New York."

"I like it," said Kira, throwing back a shot of whisky. "Get me five bars and let me see what I can do."

To make the counterfeit gold coins only required a small amount of gold, since most of the coin's weight was lead. It really wasn't a hard process if you had the dies and presses. Kira and her brothers had some of the best!

It took Kira and her brothers a week to build the drill press apparatus to drill the gold bars. She took a piece of pipe, which was very common in the mining district, and sharpened the entire edge. Using vices to hold the bar in place, she constructed a wheel and gear that slowly drilled the sharpened steel through the softer gold bar. When it was done, she had a round piece of gold the same length as the gold bar, and a gold bar with a perfectly round hole. After that, it was short work to build a form to make the plug to fill the gold bars and bring them back to within one-tenth of their official weight.

It was a Sunday morning when Kira strolled into the Wild Horse Saloon carrying a carpet bag with the five gold bars.

"Morning," Kira said to the bartender. "Is J.T. up and about?"

"Yes, ma'am. He's in his office, Miss Kira," replied the barkeep.

Kira knocked on the office door and waited a couple of seconds and then went in.

"Kira!" beamed J.T., taking in the carpet bag she was

carrying. "How about some breakfast? I just ordered mine."

"Sounds good. My Al is not a very good cook," she answered. "I'll have whatever you're having."

J.T. stepped to his office door and ordered another breakfast from the bartender.

Kira placed the carpet bag on the desk and started laughing. J.T. was rubbing his hands together like a little kid at Christmas. She took the five bars out and laid them on the desk. "What do you think?" she asked.

J.T. picked up a bar and eyed it closely. "Jeez, Kira, were you able to do anything?" asked J.T.

"I don't know. What do you think?" she said, reaching in her bag and holding up one of the gold plugs and smiling.

"Holy smokes!" exclaimed J.T. "This is even better than the coins. I can't see anything on this bar. I had faith in you, but I must say, you amaze even me."

"That would be the point, wouldn't it?" asked Kira. "Have you thought of a way to substitute our bars?"

"I was thinking about that," answered J.T. "I think I can get Powell and Tom, Jr. jobs driving one of the gold wagons from the ore processors to the U.S. Assay Offices."

"Won't it be locked with a guard?" she asked.

"Of course, but my man, Billy Braxton, will be the guard for their wagon, and he will have the key," answered J.T. smiling.

"So how we gonna split this deal?" asked Kira.

"We've been 50/50 on the eagles, so I don't see any reason to change, do you?" answered J.T. "I'll cover paying Braxton and Powell. I may have to pay a little bribe to get the boys hired on as temporaries, but we can take that out of our profits before we split."

Kira smiled. "You're always a businessman, J.T.," a crooked businessman, but who was she to throw stones. "What's the story with Braxton and Powell?" she asked. "You sure they can be trusted?"

"Oh yeah," said J.T. "They came out here from back East, probably on the run. I never asked. They are mean as hell. Anyway, they started trying to shake down some of the miners for protection. Neither had been around a mining town and they were just about to be lynched by a mining committee. I saved their bacon, and they have worked for me ever since. Trust me. I pay them good, so you can count on them doing anything we need them to."

Kira and J.T. had been in business six months, and the genuine money had literally been rolling in. Kira made coins with the gold plugs and the bar exchange process had gone flawlessly. Kira occasionally made legitimate gold bars with the excess gold. Kira knew from her uncle not to flood the market with the counterfeit coins, and they did the same with the gold bar exchanges. J.T. put her share of their spoils in the bank for her and brought back her bank book so people rarely saw her. Things couldn't be better.

WOMEN COUNTERFEITERS.

Every Gang Ever Arrested Had at Least One Female Member.

Women have a weakness for counterfeiting. The first person ever executed for that crime was a woman. She was an English woman named Barbara Spencer, and was put to death in 1721 for making false shillings. She was strangled and burned at the stake. Curiously enough, her accomplices were acquitted.

Nancy Kidd was one of the most remarkable female counterfeiters ever known in this country. She carried on her nefarious trade for more than 30 years in Chicago, and was arrested there many times. On one of these occasions a lot of fiber paper was discovered on her person.

The government officials were completely at a loss to know how she had obtained this. Finally she confessed that a chemical solution had been used to wash the faces of the notes and make them perfectly clean. Thus she was in the habit of taking one-dollar bills and changing them into large denominations.

One of the cleverest tricks ever played on Uncle Sam was invented by a woman who lived in Philadelphia. Her plan was to take $10 and $20 gold pieces, and with a small drill worked by steam power to bore out the insides and then refill them with some base metal, being very careful that they should weigh exactly the right amount when she had finished.

In this way she made $7.50 on every eagle and about $16 on every double eagle.

Women teach their husbands how to make false money. This is what happened when Ben Boyd married Mary Ackerman, of Indiana. Her father was one of the most successful counterfeiters of his day, and his daughter had a thorough acquaintance with the art. Mrs. Boyd carefully taught her husband all the secrets of the trade, and he became one of the most famous forgers of the age.

They carried on the business with such a high degree of skill that they were not captured for years, and, when at last the secret service Hawkshaws did run them down, not a single counterfeit plate, note or coin was found in their possession. When their house was searched $8,000 in good money was found.

Afterward sufficient evidence was secured to convict them and they were sent to prison. They both claimed to be converted while in state prison, and after their release settled in Chicago, where they apparently lived an honest life.

Practically every gang of counterfeiters ever arrested has had women associates. In the office of the secret service in Washington there is a large frame four feet square, filled with the

tremely wet, but not cold; winters are very long, and the feeding period will be at least seven months. The cereals will not ripen and the vegetables will not mature.—Chicago Tribune.

FRESHMAN GETS A LESSON.

Bryn Mawr Girls Teach a Sportive Harvard Youth Manners.

A Chicago young man in Cambridge found recently that he could not make fun of the women's colleges with impunity. In his letters to his sister, reports the Chronicle of that city, he had spoken of her college as an incubator several times and said he wondered when the chicks would hatch, and if they would take a postgraduate in a brooder. His sister didn't care much for that sort of thing from a brother, who was only a freshman himself, albeit a Harvard freshman, nor did the other Bryn Mawr girls, to whom she repeated his remarks.

On the day of the receipt of a letter from him saying he was coming down to inspect the "apparatus" the members of his sister's class held a meeting in her room. On his arrival, two days later, he was ushered with some ceremony into the reception-room.

After waiting 20 minutes a girl came in hurriedly, looked fairly at him and said "Oh!" Then she left abruptly. In five minutes a second girl rushed in, saying "Oh!" turned round and walked out. Five minutes later a third girl did likewise, and in another five minutes it happened again. This continued for just one hour, when all of the 24 girls that had said "Oh!" together with about as many more, all strangers, came in in a body, said "Oh!" and filed out.

Then the freshman's sister came in, by which time the youth was ready to collapse, and asked him how he liked the chicks, and if he didn't think they could peep prettily, after which she invited him to a spread in her room with the chicks, where they demonstrated they could pick up crumbs as well as peep.

PIN HOLES IN THE CHECKS.

Only One of the Cashier's Precautions Overlooked by the Forger.

In the course of a lecture delivered recently on chemical tests used in discovering by the ink the age of documents, and whether there have been interpolations, Prof. C. A. Doremus told of a curious discovery in the case of a raised check, made by his father, who is an expert in chemistry and in documents. The interests involved in this case, says the New York Sun, were very large, and it was not practicable that the original check should be tampered with or chemically treated. For purposes of testimony an enlarged photograph of the check was taken by Dr. Doremus, who was called as an expert in the case. The first trial resulted in

1899 "Steamboat Pilot" Newspaper Article, re Women Counterfeiters

CHAPTER 12

Eddie and the kids decided to walk to their destination so they could look over more of the town.

"It's really amazing what gold can do," said Eddie. "They have electricity, running water and indoor plumbing here in Cripple Creek, while that's not the case in some of the larger cities back East."

Maggie, Stephen and Lizzie didn't answer, but just exchanged looks.

"I would guess that you three are familiar with those amenities," added Eddie, not missing their looks.

"Yes, sir," said Lizzie. "But why does it smell so bad?"

"Not everybody has the amenities, so there are plenty of privies, and, of course, horses. The city, believe it or not, collects garbage once a week. They take it to an abandoned mine several miles out of town and just dump it down the shaft," answered Eddie.

"Where are you dumping us exactly?" asked Maggie.

"Easy," said Eddie. "I've already told you, I'm not dumping you. I expect you to keep your eyes and ears open and report every day. I'm just keeping us separated so nobody notices any of us together."

"Okay," said Stephen. But, what exactly is this boarding house?"

"Obviously, the town has a lot of businesses and they need

workers. Mining is a dangerous business, so there unfortunately are a lot of widows. Most are respectable, but they need jobs and don't want to end up on Meyers Avenue. This Mary Helen belongs to some kind of women's movement that helps respectable women," answered Eddie.

"That's good for Maggie and Lizzie, but what about me?" asked Stephen.

"Since I didn't know you three were coming, I'm not totally sure. But I asked around, and I think they do have kids there. It's kind of like an orphanage too," replied Eddie.

As it turned out, when they got to the address, it was more of a compound. There was a white picket fence that encompassed the entire block and four large Victorian houses. A sign out front identified the compound as "The Haven House."

"Wow," said Maggie. "This is pretty impressive."

"Let's get this over with," said Stephen, opening the gate for the others.

As they entered the house, a bell tinkled and an older woman looked up from a desk. It looked like the lobby of a hotel.

"Can I help you?" the older woman asked amiably.

"Top of the morning, ma'am," said Eddie, taking off his hat. "We're here to see Mary Helen. My name is Eddie Donnally."

"She's doing the weekly grocery order in her office. Last door on the left," she said, pointing down an adjoining hall.

"Let me do most of the talking," said Eddie, as they went down the hall. "I'm not sure exactly what she knows about the Service." Eddie gave a light knock on the partially opened door.

A lilting Irish accented voice called out, "Come in."

Eddie ushered the three kids in first and started with, "Top of the . . . ," Instead of an old grandmotherly type woman, in front of him was a slender, strawberry blonde woman with bright blue eyes and a figure that looked nothing like a potato. His merry greeting was frozen on his lips.

Lizzie, doing her usual, saved him by stepping forward and saying, "Hello, ma'am, my name is Lizzie."

Maggie gave Eddie a slight elbow and a look.

"Nice to meet you, Lizzie. I'm Mary Helen," said the woman, rising from her chair.

"This is my brother, Stephen, and my cousin Maggie. The older gentleman is our Uncle Eddie," Lizzie continued.

Mary Helen stood up and shook hands with each of them, and looked wonderingly at Eddie. "You wouldn't by any chance be 'The Eddie Donnally'?" she asked, still holding their handshake.

"Yes, ma'am. That would be me," Eddie managed to get out.

"Have a seat. Let me close the door," Mary Helen instructed. She shut the door and then cranked the transom window shut, effectively sound-proofing the room. Her resemblance to Lizzie was amazing observed Eddie as Mary Helen returned to her chair.

"I have to tell you that this was not what I expected when I got the letter from Aunt Lucy and the Chief," she began.

"You call him Chief too?" asked Eddie.

"The whole family does," said Mary Helen laughing. "It just seems to suit him."

"He's a fine man," said Eddie.

"Funny, he says the same thing about you, Mr. Donnally," she answered.

"Please, it's Eddie. I don't really answer to anything else," smiled Eddie.

The pair hadn't taken their eyes off each other. Maggie, Lizzie and Stephen exchanged looks, and Maggie cleared her throat.

"I can truly say him turning up with you three is the last thing I expected," said Mary Helen, shifting her attention and smiling at the trio.

"I expected to see Mr. Donnally, excuse me, Eddie, and his Chinese partner. You have some explaining to do Uncle Eddie," said Mary Helen, her attention switching back to Eddie. It was clear that she didn't approve of Eddie enlisting the help of kids.

Eddie, for one of the first times in his life, didn't know how to respond. "They were a surprise to me too," he stammered.

Maggie jumped in with, "We're from a long way away."

"We were sort of sent by a higher authority," said Stephen, blushing.

Mary Helen shot to her feet and placed her hands on the desk. Her stare was so intense and fierce that the three kids and even Eddie leaned back. "Don't tell me," she said, "Ace."

"Whew, that sure makes it easier," said Eddie, breaking the tension.

"Do you know Ace, too?" blurted Lizzie.

"Oh, I know the wee devil," said Mary Helen. "I wish I could talk about it with you, but that's one of the stupid leprechaun rules. There are only a few people you can talk with about one of his adventures."

"He sent the kids, I guess you would say, back, because he thought An Li and I needed a wee bit of help," said Eddie. "It's a little surprising, but with their help, we've made a lot of progress pretty easily. I, that is, we, came to you because we need a place for them to stay away from me and An Li."

"That makes sense," said Mary Helen, locking eyes with

Eddie. "Why don't you tell me what's happened so far?"

So Eddie filled her in, and the kids were able to state their part of the tale beginning with their train arrival.

When they were done, Mary Helen walked over and opened her office door. "Klara, would you take these kids and show them around? They will be staying with us for awhile."

"Excuse me," said Maggie, with authority.

"Just take a look around, please, so I can have a word with Eddie." said Mary Helen.

"Okay," said Maggie, leading the others out.

"So," said Eddie. "How did you end up way out here? You're not some kind of nun, are you?"

Mary Helen laughed, blushing slightly. "Not hardly. My Aunt Pearl ran a soup kitchen there in New York, and I used to help her when I was a kid. She was my hero. I guess I sort of followed in her footsteps. She had a real flair for organizing, so she and several wealthy ladies in New York founded The Haven House. If Aunt Pearl had been a man, she probably would have been competing with the Vanderbilts, Morgans and Rockefellers. There are three Haven Houses in New York, two in Boston, and obviously, one here. The Board was dismayed by descriptions of what was happening to families in the boom towns. I was sent out here to establish a Haven House three years ago, and it has worked out quite well," she related with pride.

"Quite well seems to be an understatement," complimented Eddie, unable to look away from those big, blue eyes.

"While I'm willing to help you and your partner, I'm also going to protect those kids," she added.

"That in itself is a big help to us. They have done good work so far and have been extremely helpful. But, having them stay with you and you keeping an eye on them is a way to keep them safe and still have them help us," said Eddie. "It's difficult for me and An Li to operate when we are worried about where they are and what they're up to. Working this case has been way too easy so far. I promise you, we are as committed as you to keeping them safe."

"Now that we agree, what do you want to do next?" asked Mary Helen.

There was a slight knock, and Klara ushered the trio back in.

"Perfect timing," said Eddie. "We need to plan where we go from here."

"I'm going to start staying around the Wild Horse and seeing if I can get even closer to the owner," said Eddie.

Mary Helen frowned. "You know J.T. Raines has one of the worst reputations around town, and that's saying something. Rumor has it that he has two thugs, Braxton and Powell, doing his dirty work."

"I'd like you kids to keep doing what you've been doing. Just hang around the vicinity of the saloon and the telegraph office. Once we find out the assay office they are using, we'll probably want to keep an eye on that too," said Eddie. "You kids need to watch out for anything unusual and try not to let them notice you. I'm sure that Braxton and Powell are probably the two guys you saw, Stephen."

"I have two guest rooms next to mine that you kids can stay in," said Mary Helen. "I'm not fond of you being out too late at night. You have to stay in the lighted areas close to the trolley lines. This can be a pretty rough town."

"We will," answered Maggie, with her fingers crossed behind her back.

"Okay," said Eddie, standing up. "I'll leave you three to get settled, and then you can go where you were before. Thanks for everything Mary Helen. We'll be in touch tomorrow morning."

The pair exchanged a lingering handshake that had the kids nudging each other.

CHAPTER 13

An Li was looking forward to meeting with the old pharmacist. Like so many Chinese, he revered his ancestors and had always liked the stories told by his grandfather, even though An Li was American through and through. His grandfather was fond of quoting Mark Twain: "Never let the facts get in the way of a good story." Of course, his grandfather always attributed it to Confucius remembered An Li, smiling to himself. Entering the pharmacy, An Li introduced himself to the middle-aged woman at the counter and asked to see the old man. An Li was dressed in a suit. While he expected this meeting to go well, he did not want anyone to see his disguise.

"He doesn't see many people, my son. I can help you with anything. There is no reason to be shy," she said smiling.

"I'm sorry," answered An Li. "I come with a message from his old friend, Xiang."

"I see. Please wait," answered the woman, disappearing into the back. She quickly returned and motioned An Li into the back room with a smile.

The old man was sitting at a work table on a tall stool. He looked up as An Li walked in and exclaimed, "Ah, you are An Li! You look just as your grandfather did when he was a young man."

An Li was speechless.

"Come, come," said the older man. "Has, how they say, cat got your tongue?"

"Thank you, honorable one," An Li finally stammered.

"Come sit. My wife will bring us some tea," instructed Chung. "I would not have expected to see you out here. Rumor has it that you are a lawyer who has joined forces with the Treasury Department."

An Li was again speechless.

The old one laughed. "We are in frequent contact with our brothers in New York by mail. The telegraph has no Chinese characters, so we exchange long scrolls. You must have some interesting stories," said the old man, his eyes twinkling.

For the next hour and a half, An Li regaled Li Chung and his wife with stories about his and Eddie's cases. Then, he even added some stories of his grandfather that Li Chung had never heard.

"I see why you are no longer a lawyer," said Chung.

"Actually, I'm still a lawyer, and I do a few things for those in the community, but the operative work is my passion," confided An Li.

"So, how may we help you with this passion?" asked Chung, as his wife removed the serving tray.

An Li went through their investigation and what information he and Eddie knew so far. He left out Maggie, Stephen and Lizzie for the lack of any way to explain them. "What we need is for the community to keep their eyes open, particularly, for a place that is not mining but should be. It doesn't take a lot of equipment, but they will need wood to fire their melting pots. I understand one of our people delivers wood."

"Correct," answered Chung. "As you see, we have electricity in town, but people still need wood for their fireplaces, and most of the small mines don't have the electricity. I will spread the word, and I am hopeful that someone may already have the information you are seeking."

"I'm staying at the Hotel Mandarin using a disguise," said An Li.

"You will move here. During the day, you can help our community, and in the night, you can indulge your passion. I will not take no for an answer," said Chung, with authority.

"You are more than I ever dreamed of," said An Li. "But no one can know my real identity or that I'm a Secret Service Operative. These people are very dangerous. We are pretty certain they have killed one man already."

"My son, Cripple Creek is a dangerous place every day, and especially at night. Your secret will be known only to me," promised Chung, speaking also for his wife.

CHAPTER 14

fter leaving the kids to settle in with Mary Helen, Eddie bought copies of three different Cripple Creek newspapers and headed to his room. He used the time waiting for An Li to read the three papers. Cripple Creek was truly a booming place with a ton of money to be made both legally and illegally. He grinned at the advertisement for counterfeit coin detectors. They were all familiar to him, and did provide a little deterrence. Ironically, one was manufactured in New York. Unfortunately, the counterfeit coins they were investigating would defeat each and every one. Additionally, messing with the gold bars required a big set of "cojones", as Miguel (Will Scott's partner in Worthy of Trust and Confidence) was always fond of saying. Big people like J.P. Morgan did not like being cheated, and there were plenty of hard men that could and would take care of their business. They didn't bother with the police or government, unless it was to their advantage.

Eddie sprang up at the slight tap on his door. An Li, still in his suit, came in with a spring in his step and a big grin.

"Geez," exclaimed Eddie. "It must have gone well with the old man."

'It went great. My grandfather, as usual, understated their friendship," replied An Li. "I told him roughly what we were looking for, and he's with us one-hundred percent. If it wasn't for the "wee one" and those kids, I'd say we could expect to make quick work of this case. The only thing is, I had to promise to be a Chinese lawyer for the community during the day."

"That's not all bad," laughed Eddie. "We'll have hundreds of eyes and ears on the prowl, and you won't have to be going around asking questions and maybe arousing suspicion. We can't cover each other's back very well here. I'm with you; if it wasn't for that darn leprechaun, we'd be on easy street. As it is, there's always that black cloud."

They were both silent for a moment, then An Li exclaimed, "Hey, how did it go with the Irish dumpling?"

"It went fine," replied Eddie, coloring slightly.

"I'm a lawyer, you know. The only time you ever blush is when there is a good-looking woman involved," laughed An Li.

"Okay, okay," said Eddie. "She wasn't an old dumpling." He filled An Li in on his meeting with Mary Helen and her knowledge of Ace.

"Hmmm," mused An Li. "That darn leprechaun. The kids seem all set, so we don't have to worry about them much. That's good."

"Yeah, Mary Helen is already like a momma bear about the kids," answered Eddie. "I'm planning on 'hanging out' at the Wild Horse tonight and gambling a little. All the games are crooked, but I'm just going to identify the one or two I want to hit hard tomorrow night. Raines has no real idea I'm of a criminal mind."

"He'll know for sure after tomorrow night," laughed An Li. "Just make sure you don't get your skull cracked before you confront him."

"I'm safe, I think. They know me a little in there, and when I start winning big, it will draw a crowd," answered Eddie. "Let's go get some lunch. I'm starving."

"Sounds good. There's an every man's cafe over on Brentwood that's supposed to be good," advised An Li. "I'll meet you there in 30 minutes or so."

It was unspoken, but they both planned to take wandering paths to the cafe just to be sure no one was following either of them.

CHAPTER 15

While An Li and Eddie were headed to the cafe, Kira and her brothers were having lunch.

"This stew is good Kira. Uncle Tom taught you how to do everything," said her middle brother, Al.

"Thank goodness we don't have to eat your cooking," said Tom. He was named after their incarcerated uncle, but he had always been called Junior. Their baby brother didn't say anything, just kept eating. Unfortunately, Nate had been a hard delivery, and as a result, he was what kindly people called slow. Kira was extremely protective of him, and he was devoted to her. He hardly ever left her side.

"Listen, Kira, after we get done this afternoon, me and Junior want to go down to the Wild Horse," said Al.

"You two know the rules. You get $100.00 each to gamble with. J.T. will cut you off and not give you any more," instructed Kira. She knew that as a favor to her, J.T. let the brothers win a little and lose a little. It was easy when all the games were crooked.

"We may be real late getting back," said Junior, slyly eyeing his brother.

"You guys get all the women you want, but don't mention this place or try to impress one of them with what we do," ordered Kira sternly.

"Okay," said Al. "Let's get busy."

The brothers left late in the afternoon with pockets of genuine ten dollar gold eagles. They were excited at having a night on the town.

After Tom and Al left, Kira sat in the rocking chair on the porch, and with Nate at her feet, began to read children's stories in the fading evening light.

By the time the brothers got to town, the Wild Horse was running wide open. There was a piano player in the back corner, and the air was punctuated by the shouts of winners and the groans of losers. Most of the winners were plants by J.T., and the losers the poor suckers who came to buy whisky and gamble. The brothers separated and began their night out.

Eddie entered the Wild Horse and eased up to the bar taking in the sights and sounds. "Hey, Mr. Donnally," said Ralph, the bartender.

"Hello," answered Eddie. "Quite a crowd tonight. I'll have a beer."

"Every night," answered Ralph. "One beer, coming up."

Eddie saw an open seat at a Faro table and quickly moved to take a seat. *(**See Appendix 1** for a full description of the Faro Gambling Table. Faro was played in almost every gambling hall in the Old West from 1825 to 1915. Cheating was prevalent enough that editions of Hoyle's Rules of Games began their faro section warning readers that not a single honest faro bank could be found in the United States.)* He bought $50.00 in chips and began to play. Eddie recognized the dealer tricks, and after thirty minutes of playing conservatively, was up $30.00. Then, picking up his chips, Eddie said, "I'm going to stretch my legs a little fellas. Good luck to all of you." He tossed a dollar coin to the dealer and started looking for another seat. Eddie found an open seat at a poker table and started with a hundred dollars worth of chips.

At a roulette wheel just to Eddie's right, Tom, Jr. was putting down bets. His hand froze in mid-air and he instantly paled.

"You alright, Tom?" asked the dealer.

"Yeah, I'm fine," stammered Tom. "I guess what I had for supper is not agreeing with me." As soon as the wheel stopped, Tom picked up his winnings and moved away from Eddie's table. He edged around so he could get a good look at Eddie. Eddie was concentrating on the poker game and never noticed Tom.

"Come on, Al. We've got to go," said Tom to his brother, who was gambling at another table.

"What do you mean? I've been winning a little bit. Besides, I thought we were going over to Miss Mildred's place," whined Al.

"Trust me," said Tom. "We've got to get back to Kira."

Once away from the saloon, Al asked, "What the heck, Tom?"

"I saw a guy in there that I think I recognized from New York. I've got to talk to Kira, but the guy looked like that darn Eddie Donnally to me," answered Tom.

"You mean that Secret Service fella that put Uncle Tom in prison? What would he be doing out here?" asked Al.

"I swear, you are stupid, Al. He's looking for us. Not us specifically, but whoever's been counterfeiting coins and bars," answered Tom. "There's no way he knows it's us, but he's already on to J.T. and the Wild Horse, else he wouldn't be in there."

"Not good. Kira's gonna be mad," muttered Al as they prodded their horses into a gallop.

J.T. made his way over to Eddie's table. "Good evening,

Eddie. How's your luck tonight?"

"Some good, some bad," smiled Eddie.

"Can I buy you a drink?" asked J.T.

'Sure," answered Eddie. "You fellas excuse me," he said to his table.

When they got to the bar, J.T. said, "Give us two of the good stuff, Ralph. Let's slide down to the end of the bar where it's a little quieter, Eddie."

Ralph brought the drinks and Eddie took a sip. "This is the good stuff!" he exclaimed, raising his glass to J.T. in a toast.

"So, what did you think of our operation?" asked J.T.

"Very impressive," replied Eddie. "I've already wired my associates. I believe we can do some business and make us both some money. Although by the looks of this place, you are already doing quite well."

"This place is good," said J.T. "But the real money will be buying gold bars here and then selling them back East."

"I couldn't agree with you more," replied Eddie, as he went back to the poker table.

CHAPTER 16

While Eddie was checking out the Wild Horse, An Li was also busy. Li Chung was introducing him to a small group of Chinese businessmen at a social meeting. The group was excited to have a lawyer in their community. One of the men had an office above his business and quickly offered it to An Li, free of charge. After a slight nod from Li Chung, An Li accepted the offer. "I hope I won't interfere with your business, Mr. Chan," said An Li.

"You will not young man. This office has outside stairs. It will be my honor," replied Chan.

"I am not going to bother our guest with additional business. He will be busy tomorrow," said Li Chung.

An Li stood up, bowed to the group, and headed for the hotel.

As soon as An Li left, Chung spoke. "My brothers, there is a problem here in the Cripple Creek District."

The men all looked at each other in alarm.

"No, it is not a Chinese problem, but it is one that is important. It seems there is a group of people that are counterfeiting gold coins and gold bars," informed Li Chung.

The group immediately began talking to each other.

Li Chung raised his hand. "Please, I ask you to be on guard, but, I have another request. Have your people listen for any talk they may overhear regarding the counterfeit coins. Also, the crooks are probably on a claim that is private but is not being worked as a mine. So, if any of your people notice anything odd, please inform me right away. Now, we have tea," said Chung, and the meeting immediately turned social again.

CHAPTER 17

Tom and Al rode hard back to the mine. Kira heard them and was at the door before they were off their horses.

"What has you two so spooked that you came back this early?" she asked. "It must be really something to make you skip Miss Mildred's."

"You're not going to believe it, but I think I saw Eddie Donnally in the Wild Horse tonight," answered Tom.

"What do you mean, you think?" Kira barked back at him.

"I'm not positive. I was only at the trial one day, but you were there every day," he answered. Tom had never understood why Kira was there every day. It wasn't like Uncle Tom wasn't guilty.

Kira was working hard to keep her temper in check. "Did you follow him?"

"No. We high-tailed it back here," answered Tom. "This fella had a beard, and he acted like some kind of businessman. If it was Donnally, I didn't want him to recognize me."

Kira calmed slightly. "You were probably right not to stay around. I don't think he would know you, but it was smart not to take a chance. If it's really him, this is something I've dreamed about. We can kill the low-down rat and dump him down a mine shaft."

"Won't that just make a bunch more of them show up?" questioned Al.

"You're right," answered Kira. "I'll have to give this some thought if it's him. First, tomorrow night we're going to be in place outside the Wild Horse to see if it's really Donnally. It may not be him, but I think this deserves a drink for luck." She went to a cabinet and took out a bottle of Irish whisky and four glasses. She poured a decent shot for Al, Tom and herself. She put a small amount in the glass for Nate. "Here's to it being Eddie Donnally." She toasted, and they all clinked glasses before downing the whisky.

While Al and Tom were getting undressed in their room, Al said, "That was kinda strange toasting to a Secret Service guy being in town."

"You're right," said Tom. "She really hates that Donnally. We all know we're breaking the law and they are trying to catch us. Believe me, I don't want to get caught, but it's part of the business."

"I'm just hoping it's not him," answered Al, climbing into bed. "I've got bad feeling about this, though."

CHAPTER 18

The next morning, Eddie, taking a circuitous route out of habit, went to the Haven House. He was whistling when he got off the street car, pleased with the night before and somewhat looking forward to seeing Mary Helen. This time, he was directed to the dining room. Mary Helen was sitting at a table with the trio.

"Top of the morning folks," beamed Eddie.

"So, tell us how it went last night, Uncle Eddie," requested Stephen excitedly.

"Whoa. I'm sure Uncle Eddie would be much more cooperative if we fed him some breakfast," interjected Mary Helen.

"Yeah, Stephen," said Maggie. "Where are your manners?"

"I was hoping I might get a little something here," smiled Eddie.

Mary Helen motioned to a lady in the kitchen. "Ellie, could you rustle up a plate for Eddie here please?"

"You want I should put in the rat poison or leave it out?" Ellie asked.

They all burst out laughing at Eddie's startled look.

"Gotcha, Uncle Eddie," laughed Lizzie.

"Hey, I might not tell you how it went last night, you keep that up," laughed Eddie back. "Actually, it went extremely well on two fronts. I worked the tables and picked out a couple that

I can take advantage of the way they are rigged and win big. I'm planning on being the biggest winner they've ever had."

"That would be the first winner they ever had," laughed Mary Helen.

"What happened with An Li? We saw a lot of Chinese people and businesses, but we didn't see him?" asked Maggie.

"Turns out the old man, Li Chung, is good friends with An Li's grandfather, Xiang, who is a real character. He loves to surprise and play tricks on everyone. Li Chung is putting the word out to look out for anything suspicious. An Li will not have to use his disguise too much and ask a lot of questions that would arouse suspicion. Unfortunately, he has to work as a lawyer for the Chinese community during the day, but we figured it's a pretty good trade-off."

"My, my," mused Mary Helen. "You two have been busy."

"Just trying to keep up with my nieces and nephew," laughed Eddie.

"We didn't have as much luck as we did the other day," said Maggie, sorrowfully.

"Hey, I made two bucks running telegrams around," said Stephen.

"The two men Stephen followed definitely work for the Wild Horse. Late yesterday, they took some man around the corner and back in the alley. They came out a few minutes later laughing," said Lizzie, making a face. "They're mean."

"We saw the poor guy stagger out of the alley a little later. They had beaten him up pretty good," said Stephen.

"Late in the afternoon, the place started getting busy, and some of the regular businesses started closing. That's when we left and came back here," added Maggie.

"I asked them to be back by dark, even though we have

street lights," said Mary Helen.

"What's the plan for today?" asked Stephen.

"I don't want to see J.T. until tonight, so I was thinking maybe we could take the train to Victor and see the sights," answered Eddie. "I was also hoping that Aunt Mary Helen would consent to being our guide."

Mary Helen locked eyes with Eddie for a few seconds and then said, "Okay. I'm in."

Eddie was shocked. He had been prepared to talk her into it.

"Here's your breakfast," said Ellie. "No rat poison."

"Thanks," said Eddie, who immediately got busy eating.

"I have to do a couple of things before we go," said Mary Helen. "I'll meet you at the front door in about thirty minutes."

As soon as Mary Helen left, the three kids all stared at Uncle Eddie.

"What?" he asked.

"We're watching you," said Maggie, pointing her finger. "You better be nice to Mary Helen. She's a nice lady."

"I agree with you one-hundred per cent!" said Eddie, still eating.

The five left the Haven House and caught a train for the fairly short ride to nearby Victor.

"Mining gold doesn't seem to be too glamorous," observed Stephen. "Those miners are always covered in dirt."

"You're not kidding," said Eddie. "I never really knew what it was like."

"Cripple Creek, where we are, is just one of the communities here," said Mary Helen. "This is really the Cripple Creek Mining District, and there are actually 12 communities in the District."

"How many people live here?" asked Maggie.

"Recent estimates say around 50,000, but I don't think anybody really knows, since it is growing so fast," answered Mary Helen. "There are 19 schools in the District. Cripple Creek had electricity before all of New York, and in 1893, there was water piped to every lot."

"I had no idea!" exclaimed Eddie.

"There are like 16 churches, only one of which is Catholic," said Mary Helen, smiling at Eddie. "We have two modern hospitals with over 40 doctors, a bunch of dance academies and a lot of music teachers. Almost every house around has a piano."

"I can play a little," said Lizzie, proudly.

"Really?" said Mary Helen. "I'll look forward to you playing at the Haven House."

"I saw all kinds of newspapers on the stands," stated Eddie.

"Yes, there are three dailies and five more that come out weekly or monthly. Most of those are specialties, like music or entertainment," answered Mary Helen.

"You sure know a lot about the District," said Stephen.

"That's my business," said Mary Helen. "The Haven House is very particular where they put their houses."

"I don't see anybody panning for gold," said Maggie.

"And you never will. That kind of prospecting is looking for free gold. Usually a river or a stream runs through a vein of pure gold close to the surface. The water carries that gold downstream and prospectors find nuggets or pan for gold dust. That's what they have in California. Up here is what's known as hard rock mining. The mining here is started with a four-foot drilling steel capped with a sharpened bit. One miner holds the drill shaft and another miner hits it with a sixteen pound sledge hammer. After each strike, the miner holding the bit turns it a quarter turn and the hammer man hits it again. It takes about two seconds between each strike. Once they have drilled a number of holes in what is called the headwall, dynamite is plugged into each hole. They detonate the charges and all the ore that is blown loose is loaded into ore carts. The person doing the loading is called a mucker, and he has to be pretty quick to load an ore cart or he gets fired. Mucking is extremely hard work."

"How do they get the ore carts out of the mine?" asked Maggie.

"The ore carts are pulled to a central point by burros, and then they are dumped into an ore bucket. Many of the burros spend their whole life underground. Some are blind because they have never seen daylight. If you go outside of town, you will see some burros that are now wild. They are from failed mines and were just abandoned to fend for themselves when the mines failed. [3]

The ore bucket is then pulled to the surface by either an electric, steam or mule-powered flywheel and pulley system. The bigger, real profitable mines use either electric or steam. There are many different levels and tunnels within each mine. People say there are 10,000 miles of tunnels under the District."

"But where is the gold?" asked Stephen.

------

[3] ***Author's Note:*** *The town of Cripple Creek currently has a herd of burros descended from those used in the mines. These burros can be seen roaming freely around the town and are considered a town treasure. The burros are free to graze wherever they please, including on lawns and in flower boxes.*

PHOTO - MINE BURRO DESCENDANTS, 2014

"It's in the ore. Once it gets to the surface, the ore is crushed and the gold is leached out. The big crushers are outside of town. The richness of the vein is based on how many ounces of gold are recovered from one ton of the ore. People say there has been 100 million dollars-worth of gold mined in the District," answered Mary Helen.

"Do they have electric lights down there?" asked Eddie.

"No way," said Mary Helen. "Miners are issued one candle for each shift. A lot of the miners try to hoard their candles, because some of their houses don't have power. Most can't afford electricity. They try and bring the unused candle home with them."

"Geez," said Maggie. "How much do those guys get paid?"

"They generally get the princely sum of three dollars a day," answered Mary Helen. "Some, like the guys that identify and follow the vein, also known as the drift, make more. The blast guys make more too, but there are a lot of accidents."

"After they recover the gold, it has to be assayed for its purity. Then they heat it and pour it into ingot molds. Those ingots are then shipped to Denver. The government buys some to use at the mint to make money. The rest is used by businesses, and many of the banks back East have huge vaults full of the gold bars."

"We got a crash course on the way out here from one of J.P. Morgan's men," said Eddie.

"So, who wants to be a miner?" asked Mary Helen.

"Get out of town!" exclaimed Maggie.

Mary Helen and Eddie looked at each other in confusion. "I take it that saying means nobody," said Eddie.

"Exactly," replied Maggie, pointing her finger.

"How many mines are there in the District?" asked Lizzie.

"That's something I don't know exactly," said Mary Helen. "But the mayor says there are 500 mines. Most claims are 10 acres. But, the Portland Mine started on one-tenth of an acre. The first shaft hit really high grade ore, but like most veins, it didn't go straight down, it went under other claims."

"That sounds like trouble," said Eddie.

"Not really," said Mary Helen. "Colorado operates under the law of apex. That law gives ownership of the vein to the claim where the vein reaches the surface or its closest point to the surface. The Portland Mine is now one of the biggest producers in the District, even though it started on only one-tenth of an acre."

"Man," said Stephen. "Talk about being lucky."

"Lucky is an understatement. They discovered a vug," said Mary Helen.

"What the heck is that?" asked Eddie.

"Well, you know what a geode is, right?" she asked. "You know a round rock that if you split it open, there are some beautiful crystals inside?"

"Okay," said Eddie.

"Well, they found a gold vug down there underground. It is a chamber with gold on the walls, the floor and the ceiling. It was surrounded by hard granite. People say you could carve huge slices of pure gold off the walls. They posted guards on each end. All the miners were hand-picked and had to strip and change into other clothes at the end of their shift. The owners feared they would carry gold out on their bodies."

"That's really cool," said Stephen. "Have you ever been down in a mine?"

"A good friend took me down in an abandoned mine to show me what conditions are like for the miners. The miners are all superstitious and think to bring a woman down in a mine is bad luck," said Mary Helen.

"How far down do the mines go?" asked Lizzie.

"The deepest so far is one-thousand feet, but gossip is that one mine is already past that," answered Mary Helen. "Cripple Creek has an active gossip line," she added laughing. "The lead miners are addicted to following the gold veins even though they don't own the mine. That's all they think and talk about is finding the vein and following it," said Mary Helen.

After lunch, Mary Helen continued showing them around Victor. She pointed out some of the richest mines and some mines that had went bust. She also pointed out the big crushers. They passed a flower vendor and Eddie bought Mary Helen and the girls small bouquets and a single bud for his own lapel.

"Sorry kid," Eddie told Stephen.

"Nothing to be sorry about," replied Stephen, clearly showing his disregard for 'flowers'.

Everyone had a fine time, and they got back to Haven House just before dinner. Eddie declined a dinner invitation saying he had to get ready for the night's festivities.

"Thanks Uncle Eddie," said Lizzie.

"Yes, it was a fine day," added Mary Helen, locking eyes with Eddie.

"It was my pleasure, ma'am," answered Eddie sticking out his hand for a handshake.

Instead, Mary Helen leaned forward, kissed him on the cheek, and then headed to her office.

"We'll see you in the morning, Uncle Eddie, and don't forget what we told you," said Maggie, pointing her finger.

'I won't," said Eddie, as he went out the door with a very red face.

CHAPTER 19

Kira had tossed and turned all night. Uncle Tom's trial kept playing in her head. She finally got up and went and sat in the rocker on the front porch until dawn. When the boys got up, she fixed pancakes, saying very little.

"Kira, I'm sorry," said Tom. "It may not be him."

"Don't be sorry," she said. "I just hope it is him."

"You don't want to just tell J.T., and he'll have Powell and Braxton take care of him?" asked Al. "They did a good job with that Klein fella. Those Secret Service fellas have a reputation."

"No," barked Kira, slamming down the skillet. "If it's him, he belongs to me, and don't forget it. Don't mention it to J.T. There was nothing I could do in New York, but out here is a different story."

The rest of the day didn't go well. Kira mis-struck several coins, something she almost never did. Tom and Al could do nothing right, and she was constantly cursing them.

"Come on, Kira," Tom said finally. "Let's just stop and cool down so we can be ready for tonight."

"All right," answered Kira. "You're right. You boys hook up the wagon late this afternoon and put the rifle in the back under a blanket with Nate."

CHAPTER 20

First thing that morning, Li Chung's wife ushered in a small man of Mongolian descent, named Gansulk. Gansulk and his family had come to Cripple Creek with other Chinese families to better their lives. Unfortunately for him, when he arrived, the only immediate family he had was him and his wife. He knew no one, and had taken a job as a mucker in the mine since he was quite strong. As soon as Li Chung heard that one of their people was working in a mine, he quickly found Gansulk other work and Gansulk had prospered. He now had a freight business delivering supplies from the train terminal to businesses in town. Gansulk had brought more of his family to Cripple Creek and had given them jobs, something Li Chung respected.

Gansulk was an expert horseman, and anytime the Chinese community had a celebration, he regaled everyone with his trick riding. He was also respected in the Chinese community for his archery skills. He freely passed his skill along to younger men, some of whom had become almost as good as Gansulk, but not quite.

"I'm sorry to pull you away from your business Gansulk," said Li Chung. They spoke in Chinese since it was their most comfortable language.

"It is not a problem. If you sent for me, I know it is something of great importance," answered Gansulk politely.

"I'm sure you have heard that a young Chinese lawyer is here in town," said Li Chung.

Gansulk nodded in acknowledgement.

"He is my friend's grandson, so he is the same to me," replied Chung.

Gansulk again nodded.

"During the day, he works as a lawyer, but at night he has another mission. In the day, he is not in danger, but at night, he may be vulnerable," informed Li Chung.

Gansulk again nodded, but then asked, "Is he the one that is spoken of in New York?"

"He is," answered Li Chung. "And I would like him protected during the night."

Gansulk nodded his agreement. "It would be my family's honor to protect this man."

"You must be as the shadow, Gansulk. It is very important that he not know we do this," said Li Chung. "He and his partner have been very successful in New York, but it is different here. It is, as they say, hard to get the lay of the land in such a short time."

"You can depend on me and my family," said Gansulk.

"I know," said Li Chung smiling. "That's why I selected you," he continued, giving a slight nod of his head to his colleague.

CHAPTER 21

That evening, Maggie, Stephen and Lizzie had a table to themselves in the Haven House dining room.

"Stephen," said Maggie. "You've been quiet all day since Eddie left, and I can almost see the wheels turning in your head. What's up?"

"Listen," answered Stephen. "I don't know why, but I just know we have to go over close to the Wild Horse and see Eddie in action. You don't need to come, Lizzie. You can stay here."

"I'm not staying here and having to explain to Mary Helen where you two are," she squeaked.

"All right," said Maggie. "I've got that feeling too, but remember, this is not some video game. These are bad people who do bad things for real."

"Mary Helen is working in her office, and I heard her ask Miss Ellie to bring her a tray," said Stephen. "As soon as Miss Ellie leaves the kitchen, we sneak out the back door, okay?"

"Okay," the other two answered.

An Li had ultimately convinced Li Chung that it would be best if he stayed at the Mandarin Hotel. An Li told him it wouldn't be good if anyone noticed two different men coming and going from Li Chung's at night. It had been a long day in the office, but rewarding. He had finalized several wills and also perfected the ownership of several properties so they could be filed with the state. They were routine lawyer things, but he knew it was helpful to the Chinese community. As it turned dark, An Li turned himself into an old man. He wanted to be close to the Wild Horse in case Eddie had unexpected trouble. A Chinese man would not be welcomed inside, but on the street, it wouldn't be a problem.

Just before dark, Kira and her brothers drove their wagon down Main Street and hitched it up several stores down from the Wild Horse. They wandered in and out of the shops, always keeping their eyes on the street and the front of the Wild Horse. Nate was holding his sister's hand. He too had suffered a bad day. Kira's constant cursing and yelling at Al and Tom had scared him. Things were not usually that way.

Meanwhile, Eddie was in the hotel putting the final touches on his disguise. He kept smiling to himself. There was nothing better than beating a con man at his own game. He touched the shamrock on a chain under his shirt for luck and headed out.

Maggie, Stephen and Lizzie were doing the same thing as Kira and her brothers, but from across the street. They were watching for Eddie to go into the Wild Horse so they could cross the street and then be able to look in the front windows.

"Stephen," said Maggie. "You see those people across the street?"

"Which ones?" asked Stephen.

"That big woman and the three men with her, you nitwit," said Maggie, slapping his arm.

"What about them?" asked Stephen.

"They are staring at the front of the Wild Horse like they are watching for somebody," she answered.

"Look," said Lizzie. "There's Eddie crossing the street."

The trio watched as Kira and her brothers fixated on Eddie.

"I got a bad feeling about this," said Stephen.

"Me, too," said Maggie. "Let's cross the street and get behind them."

As soon as Eddie stepped into the light coming from the front of the Wild Horse, Kira gasped. "That is stinking Eddie Donnally. He's not fooling me with that beard."

"Do you think he's looking for us?" asked Tom.

"No, but he has J.T. in his sights," she answered.

"See, I told you, Al," said Tom, Jr.

"What are we gonna do?" asked Al, nervously.

"Let's watch from outside and see what he's up to," muttered Kira.

As he walked into the Wild Horse, Eddie ran into J.T. "Evening, J.T.," said Eddie.

"Good evening to you," replied J.T. "These are two of my trusted employees, Braxton and Powell. The men shook hands with Eddie.

"Are those last names or first names?" inquired Eddie.

"J.T. laughed. "They're last names, but that's the only thing anyone calls them around here. Good luck tonight," he continued as the three moved away.

The Cassidys watched for the next thirty minutes as Eddie won big at a Faro table near the back of the Wild Horse. Eddie took his sizeable winnings and moved toward the poker table where he was planning to "break the bank." Two men got up, but just as he was about to take a chair, a man stepped in front of him and sat down. Unfortunately, the poker table was right in front of the big window and the only seat was one that left Eddie with his back to the window.

"Here's a seat for you mister," said the dealer, pointing to the seat Eddie didn't want.

"Looks like a lucky seat to me," said Eddie. He hated having his back to the window, but it should be alright. No one here knew or suspected that he was a Secret Service Operative.

Maggie, Stephen and Lizzie were a half-a-block behind Kira and her brothers. After a whispered conversation, there was no doubt in their mind that the group was watching Eddie.

Kira had eyes for no one but Eddie. She smiled as he won big at the Faro table. "I gotta admit. The man knows how to beat a crooked game."

"Look. He's moving," said Tom.

Kira saw Eddie get stuck in the seat with his back to the window and she started moving.

"Nate, you get up here in the wagon and you stay there, no matter what." Nate did as he was told. Kira usually didn't use that tone with him, but when she did, she meant business.

Kira reached in and pulled out the rifle.

"Kira, what are you doing?" gasped Tom.

"That low-down rat is a sitting duck, and I'm not passing up this chance," she barked.

"But, Kira," started Tom.

"Shut up and keep a watch on Nate," she ordered as she started across the street with the rifle down by her side.

Maggie, Stephen and Lizzie were momentarily speechless. "Not good," said Stephen. "I'm following her." He was crossing the street before they could stop him.

'What are we going to do?" asked Lizzie.

"There's nothing we can do," said Maggie. "But, let's find a couple of things we can throw in case Stephen needs a distraction. Whatever happens, Lizzie, we can't wait for Stephen. We have to get back to Mary Helen as fast as we can, okay?" Maggie squeezed Lizzie's hand as they looked around for something to throw.

Stephen saw Kira go between two buildings, so he slipped through a narrow parallel alley. He got to the end just as Kira started up an alley going toward the street.

Stephen hurried to the back of the same alley and could see why Kira picked this spot. It was right across from the Wild Horse, and he could clearly see Eddie's back as he started raking it in at the poker table. Stephen slipped into the alley behind Kira, who was totally focused on Eddie. Stephen had no idea what he was going to do. The woman was three times his size, and she had a rifle. As she settled into a position to shoot, Stephen moved down the alley. He felt his leg bump into something, and he grabbed it before it fell. It was a stick with bumps all along it. He felt the end and found a round knot the size of an egg. Jeez, he thought, a shillelagh!

Kira was so focused on her murderous rage at Eddie Donnally, she didn't notice anything else. She had her finger on the trigger and Eddie's back was dead in her sights. She pulled back on the trigger and then everything went black.

The roar of the rifle froze Stephen, and he was afraid he had been too late. Then he saw the other front window of the Wild Horse explode and sparks fly out from the bullet hitting one of the electric chandeliers. He turned and ran in the opposite direction.

Maggie and Lizzie were shocked at the loudness of the rifle shot and the exploding window. It was just seconds later when Braxton and Powell rushed out the front door of the Wild Horse with guns drawn.

Tom shouted, "It came from down over there, and somebody was running." He pointed away from the spot where he knew Kira was hiding. Braxton and Powell took off down the street.

The shot and exploding window started drawing a crowd.

"Come on, Lizzie," said Maggie, grabbing her cousin's hand. "Don't run. We're going to just walk around the corner and catch the street car back to Mary Helen," said Maggie.

"But what if Eddie's hurt?" Lizzie asked.

"There's nothing we can do for him. We've got to get to Mary Helen," coaxed Maggie.

An Li had been on the same side of the street but several blocks down from the Wild Horse. He fought down the urge to run toward the Wild Horse. What was done was done. So, he pretended to be an elderly Chinese man watching all the commotion. Then he got a glimpse of Eddie on his feet, so he was satisfied he had not been hit.

Gansulk had been another block back when the shot rang out. Under his Chinese robe, he had a short bow and quiver of arrows. He quickly pulled the bow out and notched an arrow. He noticed how calm An Li appeared to be, so he un-notched his bow and put it with the arrow back under his robe. Gansulk slipped into a dark spot and watched An Li slowly move away from all the commotion.

Maggie and Lizzie jumped off the street car the instant it stopped and ran full-speed to the Haven House. They burst through the front door and met Mary Helen in the hallway. They were so out-of-breath that they couldn't speak. Mary Helen grabbed their hands and hurried them down the hall to her office. The first thing they saw was Stephen in a chair panting like them and holding a shillelagh. Mary Helen shut the door and locked it.

"Catch your breath. You're safe here. But, soon as you can, I want to know exactly what's happened," she ordered. Mary Helen got each of them a big glass of water.

They gulped down the water and looked at each other.

Mary Helen was clearly not happy.

"Okay, since I'm the oldest, I'll start," said Maggie. "We wanted to see Eddie at work at the Wild Horse, so right after supper, we went over. We were across the street browsing in a couple of stores when we saw a woman and three men really watching the front of the Wild Horse. We saw Eddie cross the street and go into the Wild Horse. The woman moved up so she could see inside. She watched for awhile and then started talking to the three men. We couldn't hear them, but the lady looked really mad. She put one of the men in their wagon and took out a rifle. Stephen went across the street to follow her. I don't know exactly what happened next," she related, again becoming breathless.

"What happened is I saw this lady go down an alley directly across from the Wild Horse. I could see Eddie through one of the front windows. The lady is really big, not fat, just real big. I really didn't know what I was going to do, but I could see her sighting in on Eddie. My leg bumped into this shillelagh, so I picked it up and whacked her with it just as she pulled the trigger. Then, I took off running and didn't stop until I got back here," informed Stephen.

"Was Eddie hurt?" asked Mary Helen, alarmed.

"No," said Lizzie. "The shot went through the other front window and hit one of the chandeliers we think. That's what some people in the crowd said."

"Braxton and Powell came through the door with their guns out. The two men who were with the woman directed them away from where the woman was hiding," added Maggie. "We left and came straight here."

"That's quite a tale," said Mary Helen. "You three should've never gone to the Wild Horse without telling me."

"We didn't think you would let us go," blurted out Lizzie, ducking her head.

"You're right. I wouldn't have let you go without me!" she answered smiling. "I wanted to see Eddie at work too."

The trio was shocked.

"I was coming to get you, but you had already gone," she said. "You three seem to have a trust problem."

"Unfortunately, we didn't get to see anything," said Maggie.

"I don't think we will see Eddie tonight," said Mary Helen. "But, I think he will be here early in the morning. Let's all hit the sack for now, and we'll finish our discussion in the morning."

"Okay," the trio answered in unison. The adrenaline rush had receded, and all three were suddenly feeling extremely tired.

CHAPTER 22

The loud shot and breaking glass had frightened Nate. He pulled the blanket around him and stared.

"You stay here, Al. Lemme go see what happened with Kira," ordered Tom. Tom slowly strolled across the street ignoring the crowd that had gathered around the front of the Wild Horse. He turned down the alleyway.

Kira was sitting up, but she was clearly dazed. "What happened?" asked Tom.

"I'm not sure. I had stinking Donnally dead in my sight. I was pulling the trigger and then everything went black. Did I get him?" she asked still dazed.

"Nah, your shot went wide and through the other front window. It hit a chandelier," he said.

"Ow," said Kira, feeling just above her left ear.

"You got a big goose egg there. Somebody hit you from behind," Tom said. "You just sit here and rest for a few minutes. We steered Braxton and Powell the other way. I'll have Al move the wagon around and pick us up."

After crossing the street and giving Al instructions, Tom came back and helped Kira back down the alley to their wagon.

As soon as the window shattered, Eddie dropped to the floor. He had a small pocket gun in his coat, but he saw no reason to draw it. Braxton and Powell were out the door with guns drawn, so Eddie picked up his winnings and moved to the side of the building and away from any window. Inside, the saloon was pandemonium, and a number of the patrons quickly exited. Eddie dropped in with them and went directly to his hotel room. It wasn't thirty minutes before there was a light tap on the door. Eddie opened it and An Li slipped in.

"What happened?" said Eddie. "Could you see anything?"

"I saw the rifle fire, and the funny thing is, when Braxton and Powell came out, two men sent them in what looked to be the wrong direction," answered An Li. "Where were you inside?"

"I got stuck with my back to the other window," answered Eddie.

"That alley was dead-on where you were sitting. You were a sitting duck," mused An Li.

"That's crazy," said Eddie. "Nobody here knows us, and I'm in good with J.T. Before the shot, I had won quite a bit, and I saw Braxton talking to J.T. They were both busy staring at my play. I plan to go back around tomorrow."

"I'll see what I can learn from Li Chung and the community. Someone may hear something," said An Li. "It was quite a commotion."

"Sounds good," said Eddie. "I'll go straight to Haven House in the morning, but I'll check to make sure I'm not followed."

"It's about time I met this Mary Helen," laughed An Li.

"Not tomorrow," replied Eddie. "I don't want anyone following me to identify you."

Back at the Wild Horse, J.T. was sitting at a table with Braxton and Powell. "What the hell just happened, J.T.?" asked Braxton with a scowl.

"I'm not sure. It may have been a sore loser trying to cause trouble," answered J.T.

"The real trouble is going to be when we catch up to the no-count that blew out that window," said Powell.

J.T. had closed the place down early, and Ralph, the bartender, was sweeping up glass, which had sprayed everywhere.

"You guys hit the street and see if some jackass is bragging around about shooting us up," instructed J.T. "If you find him, you know what to do -- and, if you can make him suffer, that's even better."

"We'll let you know as soon as we find out anything," said Braxton, as he and Powell headed out a side door looking for trouble.

CHAPTER 23

While the kids went to sleep feeling safe at Haven House, Mary Helen could not. She knew Eddie wasn't hurt, but she still fretted. She had felt a connection with Eddie Donnally the moment they met. It's just cause he's Irish and from New York she told herself. She didn't have time right now for a man in her life. Besides, Aunt Lucy had told her that Eddie was quite the ladies' man. Eddie Donnally was black Irish, dark hair, blue eyes, and the type her grandmother had always warned her about. She certainly didn't need any part of that. Mary Helen had come out West to get away from New York. She had been engaged to a blue blood who made it clear that after they were engaged, he didn't want her to have anything more to do with Haven House. His philosophy was to let the poor take care of themselves. That ended it for Mary Helen. She had jumped at the opportunity to come to Colorado. Eventually, she fell asleep, but tossed and turned all night.

The next morning, Eddie was up and out early. He walked several blocks, doubling back frequently, and then catching a trolley away from Haven House. He switched cars and caught one headed toward the Meyers Avenue red light district. He got off just short of Meyers Avenue when he saw a trolley headed toward him in the distance. At the corner stop, he hopped off and crossed the street just as the other car arrived.

He got on the trolley headed in the other direction, and nobody tried to duplicate his actions. For the rest of the ride, and up until the trolley reached a stop a few blocks from the Haven House, Eddie pondered the last night's events. Unfortunately, he didn't reach any conclusions.

Eddie entered the Haven House with the unusual expectation of seeing Mary Helen. He found her and the three kids sitting at a table in the staff dining room.

"Top of the morning, everyone," greeted Eddie.

The kids brightened and said, "good morning," in unison.

Mary Helen gave him a silent glare. Eddie came to the table and Mary Helen said, "Ellie, please bring Mr. Donnally a plate, with rat poison!"

Eddie was speechless -- an unusual condition for him.

"We're glad to see you're alright," said Lizzie.

Eddie started to reply, but Mary Helen interrupted. "Let's wait and talk to Uncle Eddie in my office."

"No problem," answered Stephen, showing his new shillelagh to Eddie.

"Wow," exclaimed Eddie, taking the cane. "This is a nice one, Stephen. You know, these are made from the blackthorn root, and they only come from Ireland. Where did you come by this?" he asked.

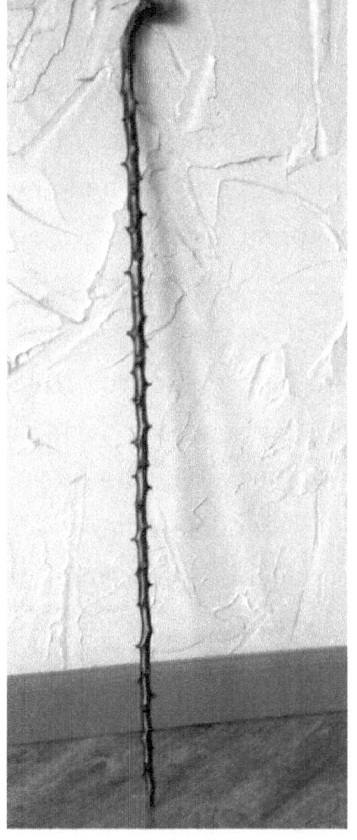

Photo Genuine Irish Shillelagh, made in Ireland from the Black Thorn Root.

"I'll wait and tell you in the office," Stephen replied, as their food arrived.

They all made short work of their meals since they were all eager to get to the office. Eddie hoped Mary Helen was joking when she ordered his with rat poison, but her glare had been unsettling.

When they got to Mary Helen's office, she locked the door and closed the transom.

Eddie said, "Something has obviously happened that I'm not aware of."

"I'll say," answered Mary Helen. "Let me summarize. Our three young friends here took it upon themselves to go over to the vicinity of the Wild Horse so they could see you in action last evening. They left without telling me or I would have gone with them. When they got there, they saw three men and a woman watching the front of the place. From the way they acted, our group believes they were closely watching for you. The woman appeared especially not to like you. She proceeded to take a rifle from their wagon and position herself in the alley directly across from the Wild Horse. Just as she was about to shoot you in the back, Stephen whacked her on the head with his shillelagh there. Then, all three skedaddled back here."

"This is extremely serious," snapped Eddie, consternation on his face.

"You're damn right, Eddie," said Mary Helen. "It's one thing for these kids to be a lookout for you, but exposing them to gunfire is just not acceptable." She locked eyes with Eddie with a glare so intense that he almost had to look away.

"I agree with you one hundred percent," said Eddie. "But, if Stephen hadn't used that shillelagh, I'd probably be at the undertakers. Where did you get that from, anyway, Stephen?"

Eddie looked to Stephen, glad to be able to look away from Mary Helen.

"I was going down the alley looking for something to hit that lady with and bumped into this shillelagh," he said, handing it to Eddie. "It's sure a nice one, and looks old."

"Do you think Ace left it for him?" asked Maggie.

"I suppose so," replied Eddie. "I can't think of any other explanation. An Li was coming up the street when the shot went off, and he saw two men direct Braxton and Powell away from the alley. It appeared to him that they all knew each other, which was a little odd since the shot was meant for me. Can you describe the three men and the woman?" he asked, taking a small journal out of his jacket pocket.

"Something seemed to be wrong with the younger one," said Lizzie. "He was holding the woman's hand and seemed to be a special needs person."

"A special needs person?" asked Mary Helen, raising her eyebrows.

"Where we're from, it's not polite to call someone retarded or slow," said Maggie.

"I see," she said, glancing at Eddie.

"Let's start with the wagon. Was it one horse or two?" asked Eddie.

"One," said Stephen. "And it was a pulled by a dark brown mule, just like a lot of the hauling wagons you see around."

"Did they seem like a family?" asked Eddie.

"I think they were definitely family, but the lady was in charge," answered Maggie.

"So, tell me what this lady in charge looked like," said Eddie, suppressing a smile, as he glanced at Mary Helen.

"She looked like a man," said Lizzie. "I mean she was

wearing a dress, but she was built like a block."

"Taller than Mary Helen?" he asked.

"Yeah," said Stephen. "Not quite as tall as you, but taller than Mary Helen."

Eddie walked the kids through a description of the other three, who they believed to be brothers. Maggie said they sort of looked alike from what they could see. When Eddie appeared to be done, Mary Helen asked the kids to go see if they could give Ellie a hand in the dining room.

"Man, I'd like to be a fly on the wall in there," said Stephen, as soon as they were in the hall.

"Oh no, not me," said Lizzie.

"Yeah," said Maggie. "Did you see how she was glaring at him?"

They continued to the dining room.

After the kids left, Mary Helen didn't say anything, but stared at Eddie.

Eddie squirmed, "Look, Mary Helen, I had no idea anybody knew we were on this case."

"I know," said Mary Helen. "I was mad at first, but if they hadn't been there . . .," she didn't finish. "Actually, it's that little leprechaun I'd like to tar and feather."

"You're not kidding," said Eddie, glad to be off the hook. "This has now become extremely dangerous. An Li and I were discussing this case on the train and wondered if it wasn't someone from back East that was doing this work. They are probably from New York and obviously know me. They probably don't know An Li, but they know I'll have a partner somewhere in town. It's very unusual that a counterfeiter would be so aggressive as to try and kill me. The best thing would be for them to just move their equipment to another area."

"So, what do you have in mind?" asked Mary Helen.

"First, I'm going to wire the Chief with the descriptions the kids gave me. I'm also going to send the counterfeit coin to D.C. and ask them to compare it to the known counterfeit coins from prior cases in New York. This stuff is just too good to be made by a first-timer. They have to keep making new planchetts because constantly striking coins wears them out," said Eddie.

"I'm not sure I understand the last part," replied Mary Helen.

"Sorry," said Eddie. "I was thinking out loud a little bit. These coins are made using hand-engraved dyes or what they call planchetts that look like the coin. They then use a press apparatus that imprints the counterfeit with what's on the die. When the planchetts get worn, the counterfeit coins are no longer sharp and distinct and can be identified pretty easily, so you have to keep making new ones."

"Okay," said Mary Helen. "But, what are you going to do with the kids?"

"They seem to be doing okay hanging around the telegraph office and wandering around town," shrugged Eddie.

Mary Helen leaned forward and locked eyes with Eddie. "That leprechaun may have sent them here, but they are now our responsibility, and don't you forget it," she ordered.

"I understand and agree," said Eddie. "I think they will be safer just carrying on with what they have been doing. Nobody would ever suspect them to be with me."

"Even so," said Mary Helen. "I'm going to have them check in with me periodically, and I can go over there and check-up on them occasionally. Everyone in town knows that we look after orphans here."

"I'll see An Li tonight and fill him in," said Eddie. He stood up to go and stuck out his hand to shake with Mary Helen.

"Thanks for looking after the kids. Its one less thing I have to worry about."

Mary Helen took his hand and held it for several seconds, looking directly into his eyes.

"Well," said Eddie, pulling back his hand and coloring slightly.

"I'll tell the kids," said Mary Helen. "And, you get going. I can't have you associated with Haven House."

CHAPTER 24

Kira hadn't slept well between the headache and the knot on her head. She couldn't get comfortable. Tom had made breakfast for everyone, and she was grateful.

"Good job, Junior," she said. "I may get you to cook more often."

"So, what are you thinking?" asked Al.

"I think I made a mistake. I let my anger get in the way of thinking up a plan. We could pack up everything and move over toward Victor, but that's a lot of trouble, and we have a good set-up here. Donnally is sure to have at least one partner, maybe more. He's still going down a mine shaft, but we need to get them both, and then just lay low for awhile," finished Kira.

"Are you going to talk to J.T.?" asked Tom.

"No. Not right now. We'll just let Donnally work his way in with J.T.; that way we know where he is and what he is doing," answered Kira.

"How are we going to find his partner?" asked Al.

"We're going to take a page out of their book and watch the hotel and follow him when he goes anyplace but the Wild Horse," said Kira.

"Those guys are really sneaky, Kira. Remember, they got Uncle Tom by following him," said Al.

"I know," she answered. "But, he doesn't really know you and Tom. I want you guys to hire some of the girls from Miss

Mildred's place and use them to help you follow him. Change out the girls every day and don't let them go out dressed like ladies of the evening. You two can follow some, but those operatives can really remember faces, so don't let them see you much."

She handed them a sack of gold coins to pay the girls. "Don't be stingy with Miss Mildred," she ordered. "These girls will be unavailable most of the day."

"Are these yours?" asked Al, lifting the bag.

"No. You know all my coins are going to J.T.'s brother in Victor. I swear sometimes I think you're as dumb as a mine burro," growled Kira. "That's just what we need -- Miss Mildred kicking up a fuss." While Kira was confident that her gold pieces would not be detected, she was not taking any chances.

As Eddie was leaving the Haven House, Tom and Al were already sitting in Miss Mildred's private office.

"So, you want to take four of my girls every day for awhile, and they don't have to do anything but follow this guy around."

"This is a really sneaky rat," said Tom. "We can't let him know he's being followed."

Mildred leaned forward and said, "alright, ten dollars a day for each girl and $100 to me for putting up with all this."

"Jeez," whined Al. "That's pretty steep."

"It's cheap," replied Mildred. "Not all of these girls are smart enough to do it. Besides, if they work all day for you, they can't work at night for me too."

"Deal," said Tom, sticking out his hand.

"Deal," said Mildred, taking Tom's hand. "But, I'll take my hundred now."

Tom and Al hustled out of town to let Kira know they had made a deal.

CHAPTER 25

When he got back to his room, Eddie got busy. He went to his traveling bag, and from underneath the lining, he pulled out his code wheel. The wheel was actually two heavy pieces of paper with numbers and letters printed on them. One of them had a window cut in it, and whatever letter you decided to put in the window determined the code. Every operative had one, and each one had the numbers and letters placed differently. All the operative had to do was let D.C. know what letter was in the window and they could decipher the message. It was very effective and could be changed with every message or in the middle of any message. It took him almost two hours to code his telegram describing the woman and maybe her brothers. Unfortunately, the description wasn't a lot, but considering the circumstances, it was pretty darn good. Those kids are sharp thought Eddie, and there's no doubt Stephen saved my hide.

Cripple Creek actually had telephone service, but the calls would go through switchboards and conversations could be listened to by nosy operators.

Eddie wrapped the counterfeit gold coin for shipment to D.C. Jim Knox, at headquarters, had started a library of specimens of known counterfeits. Eddie was convinced that this wasn't the bunch's first time making counterfeit. Maybe Jim could see some similarities between this coin and those from a previous case.

Eddie left the hotel and caught a trolley down to the Midland Train Terminal. He didn't want to use the telegraph office by the hotel. The telegram he was sending was a nonsense jumble that might be talked about by a telegraph operator. Besides, the Wells Fargo shipment office was in the train station.

After the station, Eddie headed for the cafe he and An Li had used before. Being sociable with the waitress and a couple of the local fellas, he picked up a lot of gossip about the shooting the night before.

"I heard it was some sore loser," said a guy, named Abe.

"He better hope Braxton and Powell don't find out who did it," said Polly, the waitress. "Those two are mean as rattlesnakes."

"They will have a long list of losers to choose from," said Abe. "I've never heard any good things about their games."

"You think they are rigged?" asked Eddie.

"Whoa now. I'm not saying anything like that, mister. I don't need Braxton and Powell paying me a visit!" exclaimed Abe. "Jeremiah Klein left the Wild Horse with those two one night and hasn't been seen since."

While Eddie was finishing his lunch, the coded telegram was delivered to Doris, the Chief's secretary in Washington, D.C. She opened it and then went in the Chief's office and closed the door. The Chief was out and wouldn't be back for several hours. The Chief had given her his safe's combination for just this kind of situation. She removed the Eddie Donnally wheel and began deciphering the telegram.

When the Chief got back several hours later, he stopped short when he saw Doris' face.

"Oh no. I don't like that frown on your face," he said.

"You got a telegram from Eddie, and I guess it's good, but

not good," she replied.

The Chief sat down next to her desk. "I'll read it, but why don't you just fill me in on its contents right now."

"It seems he and An Li thought they were making good progress, but last night someone tried to shoot Eddie in the back. Given that, he now believes it's somebody from New York that is doing the counterfeiting. He figures they recognized him from a previous case, but he has no idea who it might be. He sent a description of four suspects, three men and a woman. It's not great, but one of the men is probably retarded, and the woman, who appears to be in charge, is quite large. In fact, she's the one who tried to shoot him," informed Doris, speaking rapidly.

"Good Lord!" exclaimed Chief Bell. "That's why I hand-selected Eddie and An Li. I thought they would be unknown way out there."

Doris, being a devout Catholic, colored slightly at the Chief's expletive. "He's also sending the counterfeit coin by Wells Fargo Express, and he wants Jim Knox to examine it and see if it matches anything in his library."

The Chief stood up. "I'm going downstairs to talk to Jim."

"You don't want to read the telegram?" she asked.

"You've told me enough. I'll read it for myself when I come back," he answered.

Jim Knox's office was not really an office. It was a very large vault. Along the walls, he had an impressive number of samples of counterfeit gold and silver coins, as well as paper currency. He also had mug shots and case histories going back about 20 years.

"Afternoon Jim," said Chief Bell.

"Hey, Chief," answered Jim laughing.

TREASURY DEPARTMENT.
S. S. D.   Form 8.

No.

Description of

Caterina Caurina

alias

Taken *December*, 19**0**9
Residence,
Legit. occupation,
Crim. occupation, *cft do to prener*
Nationality, *Italian*
Age, ; Height,
Weight, ; Build,
Complexion, ; Eyes,
Hair, ; Beard,
Peculiarities, etc.:

When arrested, *Dec 10/09*
Where arrested, *Wilkes Barre Pa*
When sentenced, *January 2/10*
Length of sentence, *One year*

PHOTO AND ARREST CARD OF WOMAN COUNTERFEITER

TREASURY DEPARTMENT.
S. S. Div.—Form 8.

87-C-161

No. *1007*   Description of

Mrs Vemo Luty

alias

Taken _9/3 1904_ , 18
Residence, _Duquesne Pa_
Legit. occupation, _______
Crim. occupation, _Counterfeiter_
Nationality, _Am_
Age, _h_ ; Height, _5'7_
Weight, _120_ ; Build, _Slender_
Complexion, _dark_ ; Eyes, _Black_
Hair, _Black_ ; Beard, _______
Peculiarities, etc.: _______

When arrested, _9/3 1904_
Where arrested, _Duquesne Pa_
When sentenced, _9/22 1904_
Length of sentence, _1 year H. l._

PHOTO AND ARREST CARD OF WOMAN COUNTERFEITER

"I know it sounds funny to me too," said Bell. "I messed up, Jim, and I'm hoping you can rescue me. Eddie and An Li are in Colorado working on the gold bar scam, as well as a counterfeit gold Eagle case. I should have had you take a look at that coin before I sent them out there. Someone took a shot at Eddie last night. He's alright, but he and An Li both believe it was probably someone from New York who is out there and recognized Eddie from a previous case."

"Did they get any descriptions?" asked Knox.

"Some," answered the Chief. "It was three men and a woman. One of the men is probably retarded, and the woman is the one who fired the shot. They described the woman as big, not fat."

Knox leaned back in his chair. "Unfortunately, it doesn't ring a bell, but I'll look at some of the New York case files to see if something clicks."[4]

"Eddie is sending the coin back by Wells Fargo express, so you should have it by tomorrow afternoon," informed the Chief.

"Great. I'll get right on it," said Knox.

"Thanks, Jim. I'm going to send a message to all the offices, making sure they forward you at least one sample of any counterfeit coins or currency they recover," said the Chief, rising to leave.

"Most of them are doing it now," said Jim. "But, it would be great if it was a standard procedure."

---

[4] ***Author's Note:*** *To this day, The Secret Service maintains an extensive library of known counterfeit money. As soon as a new counterfeit is detected, the Field Office is required to send in samples to the Washington, D.C. Headquarters' library.*

"Consider it done," answered Bell. Chief Bell stopped outside Knox's office and took a look at a board containing pictures of known women counterfeiters. There were a surprising number of them. Unfortunately, after ten minutes of looking, he concluded none of the women even resembled the woman in Cripple Creek. Sighing to himself, he headed back upstairs to push some paper.

CHAPTER 26

After lunch, Eddie took a slow stroll around several blocks and then went to the Wild Horse. There were several men busy installing a new front window. Eddie went to the front door and realized the place had a fair number of patrons drinking and gambling, despite last night's commotion. Before Eddie could make it to the bar, he saw Braxton.

"Afternoon, Mr. Braxton," said Eddie.

"The boss wants to see you in his office. You were quite the big man last night," grumbled Braxton.

Braxton ushered Eddie into J.T.'s office and shut the door on his way out.

"Afternoon, J.T.," said Eddie, taking a seat.

"Hey, Eddie. Good to see you. That was quite the commotion we had last night," gushed J.T.

"Yeah, it interrupted my winning streak," complained Eddie.

"That's what I wanted to talk to you about," said J.T., coming around and sitting in the chair next to Eddie. "You been holding out on me? I thought you might be an honest businessman, but after your performance last night, I know better," said J.T.

"Let's just say I'm a businessman, but I am the front man for a New York Irish syndicate. That is the whole truth, so help me God," laughed Eddie. "It's not so hard to best a crooked game when you recognize the method being used."

"One of my games rigged -- I'm offended," laughed J.T. "How about a drink of the good stuff?"

"Sure," said Eddie, "if it's Irish whisky."

"That it is," said J.T., going to a bar against the wall and pouring whisky into two glasses from a cut glass decanter.

"How come you showed up at my place, Eddie? There are a lot of saloons and gambling houses in the District," said J.T., somewhat suspiciously.

"You know you have a reputation, not a bad one to a man in my business, and you grew up in the District. There's probably not much goes on here that you don't know about," mused Eddie.

"You're probably right," said J.T pointedly. "But, how did you know?"

"Oh, you remember about six months ago when that circus was in town?" asked Eddie. He had seen the circus flyers still posted on poles and the sides of buildings around town and decided to use it to his advantage.

J.T. nodded.

"There's quite a group of my Irish brethren that run that affair," said Eddie.

J.T. laughed. "There were some silver items missing from around here. Not too much to cause an uproar, but a nice little haul."

"That's my lads," said Eddie. "A little here, a little there. By the way, said Eddie, reaching into his coat pocket. "Here's the money I won last night. I'm not going to take money from a man I want to do business with." Eddie pulled a sack of gold coins from his pocket and emptied them on the small table between them.

Shocked, J.T. stared at the money for several seconds before taking it. "I don't mean to offend you, but you are a gentleman," said J.T., as he raised his glass to Eddie.

Eddie laughed, "I've been called a lot of things from time to time, but gentleman does not come up very often." Eddie was ecstatic inside. His and An Li's ploy had worked to perfection. This was one of the trickiest parts of an operation, where there was no introduction by another criminal. He and An Li had decided that giving back the money would smooth over any mistrust by J.T. and convince him of Eddie's criminal intentions. Eddie could barely keep from laughing. He could practically see the dollar signs in J.T.'s eyes when he saw his money being returned.

"So, what do you fellas have in mind?" asked J.T, rubbing his hands together, any suspicions long gone.

Eddie reached in his jacket again and pulled out a piece of heavy folded paper. He unfolded it and laid it on the table between the chairs. "I'm sure you know what this is," said Eddie.

"Of course," said J.T. "That's a share certificate for one of the gold mines in the District."

"Look close," instructed Eddie.

J.T. picked up the share certificate, held it up to the light, and read the company name. "I don't notice anything," said J.T., handing it back to Eddie.

"That's good," laughed Eddie. "It's counterfeit!"

"Lemme see that," barked J.T. He looked close again. "Could've fooled me."

"That's the whole point," said Eddie.

"How do you make money?" asked J.T.

"It's pretty easy," said Eddie. "Do you ever have anything to do with the Cripple Creek Gold and Mining Exchange?"

"No. I got my own gold exchange going here," said J.T. laughing. "Take a look at this." J.T. went to his desk and pulled out a 16 ounce gold bar. He handed it to Eddie.

"I guess there are a lot of these gold bars around here," said Eddie, who was again ecstatic inside.

"Not like this one," bragged J.T. "There are about six ounces of gold and 10 ounces of nickel and lead to make it weigh properly."

"Wow. You wouldn't believe what I could do in New York with a bunch of these!" exclaimed Eddie.

"There is a big shipment being prepared, but after that, we can talk," responded J.T.

"My counterfeit stock certificates seem pretty tame compared to that," praised Eddie.

"Let me hear about your stock scheme anyway," said J.T., proud of himself.

"Well, at the Gold Mining Exchange and at the New York Stock Exchange, you can deposit paper shares into an account and they will hold them for you in their vault. If the stock price goes up, you make money, and if it goes down, you lose. They also buy and sell stock certificates themselves. If you go in there, you will see a chalkboard with buy and sell prices. Those prices can change during the day. If you go in there with stock certificates, they will buy them and pay you right there in cash. Nobody really knows how many shares there are in some of these big outfits. The owners may know, but there is no way to monitor what is out there. You just have to have different people go in with stock certificates for different companies. It's quick and painless if you don't get too greedy and try to cash in too many shares at once."

PHOTO - GOLD MINE STOCK CERTIFICATE.

"I like it," said J.T. "You need me to get people to take in your certificates and bring back the cash."

"Right," answered Eddie. "But, we also need some muscle to keep the people in line. I'm sure you have people that owe you money and would like to get out from under. Your boys, Braxton and Powell, would escort the runners to the stock exchange and then escort them back here with the proceeds."

"So", said J.T. "How do you propose to split these proceeds, 50-50?"

Eddie frowned. "How are you splitting with the gold bar people?" he asked.

"I'm 50-50," said J.T. "But we've been friends a long time."

"My end requires a lot of skill and is expensive," continued Eddie. "I had 70-30 in mind."

J.T. didn't answer. After thinking awhile, he smiled, "Make it 60-40 to you and you've got a deal."

"Done," said Eddie, sticking out his hand to shake on it.

"Done," said J.T. "But, please don't gamble here anymore."

"I won't," laughed Eddie. "I've got other things to do. I have to wire New York and tell them what's happening. I'll go to the Gold Mine Exchange tomorrow and buy a few shares of some big company's stock. Then I have to send them to New York. It normally doesn't take long to get the printing done. Half the time, many features are the same, just a different name. I'd say we should be ready to go in no less than two weeks, maybe sooner."

"That's good," said J.T. "I'm right in the middle of something with my gold partners."

Eddie pulled out his pocket watch and said, "I think I'll go over and watch a little business at the Gold Exchange before I start buying myself."

"Come in for a drink anytime," said J.T., as he escorted Eddie out of his office.

CHAPTER 27

Eddie wandered into the stock exchange and was impressed. It was every bit as big and as busy as the New York Stock Exchanges. He watched as the price fluctuated on some of the newer stocks. Shares of the Prospect and Independence Mine, two of the largest, stayed steady. Those mines were older, deeper and owned and controlled by big corporations back East. Eddie was interested in the stocks that were volatile. Their shares would fluctuate on rumor and speculation of the quality of the ore they were producing. Once the mine proved to be a good one, the syndicate bird dogs bought a big chunk of shares and promptly fired the owners, or worst of all, kept them on at $3.00 a day. The syndicates cancelled the contract with the Stock Exchange since they were the new owners and no new shares were issued. The shares held by the miners were so few that they were virtually worthless no matter how profitable the mine. The syndicates usually bought the miners' few shares for a pittance. J.P. Morgan's man had told them all about it on the train. Always rooting for the underdog, it really galled Eddie.

Eddie decided to go ahead and buy a few shares of a half dozen mines just in case anyone was watching him. An Li could easily fill in the mine names and number of shares, but Eddie hoped it would never come to that. They had two weeks to find out who was supplying J.T. with the ingots and the coins. Eddie left the exchange and grabbed his usual three papers, then headed back to the hotel to wait for his rendezvous with An Li.

Eddie was sitting in the hotel parlor sipping an Irish coffee when An Li strolled in.

"My, you're a sight," said Eddie, eyeing An Li's suit and tie.

"I decided a Chinese lawyer showing up at the front door would be better than an elderly Chinaman sneaking up the back stairs," answered An Li.

"You're probably right," said Eddie. "Well, I made some good progress today. J.T. bought my swindler act all the way. You should have seen his face when I gave him the money back. I swear I saw dollar signs in his eyes. He showed me one of the gold bars, so we are definitely in the right place."

"How long do we have?" asked An Li.

"I told him it would take at least two weeks to get the stock certificates back from New York. But, I went ahead and bought a few shares from the Gold Exchange just in case," answered Eddie.

"You get any hint of who they are working with?" asked An Li.

"Nah," said Eddie. "He was close-mouthed, but he did say he was working on a big gold bar deal and then he would be ready to go with me. He let slip that he has known the counterfeiters a long time."

"We can try to surveil J.T. with me, the kids and probably Mary Helen," said An Li.

"You and the kids," mused Eddie. "But Mary Helen may be too well-known around town. And, I think she will be like a wounded bear if we try to involve the kids any more than they already are."

"C'mon, Eddie, can't you use some of that Irish charm you're so famous for?" said An Li, laughing.

"I can try. I think she will be okay using them in the daytime, but at night is going to be a problem. Although, the other night the kids saved my bacon, for sure," stated Eddie. "I can get some miner's clothes and maybe change at the Haven House, and we can watch the Wild Horse at night. J.T. doesn't leave much, and Braxton and Powell seem to be the muscle there every night."

"So, you'll talk to Mary Helen in the morning then?" asked An Li.

"Oh no!" exclaimed Eddie. "We will meet with Mary Helen in the morning and try to enlist the kids for the daytime work."

"All right," answered An Li. "I'll be there by 9:30 a.m."

"Don't worry, I'm not starting without you." said Eddie.

"I'll go change and wander around a little bit tonight. I've got Li Chung asking around about the three men and the woman. He thinks someone is bound to have noticed them. The Chinese service just about everything in town," said An Li, standing up.

"Go with God my son," said Eddie, making the sign of the cross.

An Li just shook his head and left with a grin on his face.

Eddie just stared at his paper after An Li left. "What are you up to Ace?" he asked aloud. "The kid saved me for sure, but they are still here. That is a worry that I can do nothing about. For God's sake, don't let any of them get hurt. Mary Helen McDougal would certainly kill me." Eddie shrugged to himself and went back to reading his papers.

CHAPTER 28

Tom had decided to scout the area around the hotel and the saloon for good observation spots. He couldn't believe his luck when he saw Eddie Donnally walking across the street. Tom decided to watch Eddie just to see how he acted. Eddie was visible in the hotel parlor window, and to Tom's astonishment, he saw a Chinaman walk in and start talking to Eddie. Just by watching them, he could tell they were friends. He whistled to himself. That stinking Donnally's partner is a Chinaman. Wait till I tell Kira he thought as he hurried to the livery stable to get his horse. Tom pushed his horse all the way to their claim. He quickly tied him and hurried into the mine.

Kira was at work with Al coring gold bars.

"What's happening?" asked Kira. "You look like the cat that got the canary."

"That's because I did," beamed Tom. "I went back to Miss Mildred's and got that all set for tomorrow. But, I decided to go over by the hotel and the Wild Horse to make sure I had some good viewing spots. Lo and behold, I saw that stinking Donnally walking across the street to the hotel."

"Get on with it, will you?" barked Kira, anxiously.

"I think I know who his partner is," answered Tom. "You won't believe it, but I think it is a Chinaman."

"What?" said Kira, unbelievingly.

"I saw a Chinaman wearing a suit walk in and sit down with Donnally big as you please. I could tell they knew each other well. There was no hand-shaking or any of that stuff. They just started talking," informed Tom.

"A Chinaman!" exclaimed Kira. "Don't that beat all?"

"So, we gonna tell J.T. and get Braxton and Powell to help us throw them down a mine shaft?" asked Al, hopefully.

"By God, no!" barked Kira, again. "I told you Donnally is mine. Besides, we've got this big shipment to get out. After that, we can take care of Donnally and this Chinaman. But, I still want Donnally followed. He's one sneaky no-count. There may be more than just the two of them."

"Okay," said Tom. "The girls are lined up, and we will be out there early.

"It will be interesting to see just what Mr. Stinking Eddie Donnally is up to," growled Kira. A Chinaman -- what is the world coming to? she thought to herself.

CHAPTER 29

Eddie was up early and looking forward to seeing Mary Helen again. She was a good-looking woman and would make somebody a fine wife he thought. That thought was immediately followed by what the heck are you thinking? He was flattered that she seemed to like him, but he lived in New York and she was way out here in the West. What kind of a relationship could they have, he continued to himself.

Eddie left the hotel headed for the trolley. He was carrying a travel bag with the blank stock certificates and the counterfeit gold bar. He was certain that his room would be searched, and he didn't want any of this found. Out of habit, he walked a block or two then doubled back before taking the trolley. The streets were crowded, and he didn't notice the couple of ladies across the street who were watching him. While Eddie got on the front of the trolley, two of Miss Mildred's girls got on in the back. Eddie got off at the trolley stop just around the corner from Haven House. His mind was on Mary Helen, and he didn't notice the two women who also got off. One of the girls followed Eddie about a half a block back. She turned the corner just in time to see Eddie go up the steps at Haven House.

The girl turned and went back the way she came. She sent the other girl to a store across the street that had a view of the Haven House. It wasn't 15 minutes before An Li got off the trolley and made his way to Haven House.

An Li entered Haven House, and before he could speak, Klara just pointed down the hall to her right and said, "The Irish devil is down there with Mary Helen in her office."

An Li's face broke into a grin as he hurried to Mary Helen's office. He gave a light knock and went in when Eddie called out. "Good morning, ma'am. You must be Mary Helen," said An Li. He wasn't surprised at her prettiness. He could read Eddie like a book. "You are as pretty as Eddie said," he continued.

"Good morning, yourself. And what blarney has Eddie been telling you?" she asked as she eyed Eddie's discomfort with pleasure. "Let's sit down," invited Mary Helen. "With two of you showing up, I know its trouble."

"We both knew it was going too easy. That being said, we now know definitely that J.T. Raines is heavily involved. We would like to use the kids in the daytime to keep an eye on the Wild Horse. They may have to follow Braxton or Powell some," stated Eddie.

"I don't know, Eddie," Mary Helen answered locking eyes with him. "You know those two have a bad reputation in a rough town. They won't have any mercy, even on a kid."

An Li chimed in, "We have the same reservations. We can give them a crash course in tailing someone and impress on them how important it is to let the quarry go if things get tight."

"I guess I can give them a hand," said Mary Helen, thoughtfully.

An Li and Eddie looked at each other. "Actually, Mary Helen, you're probably too well known around town. Your being there could actually make the situation more dangerous. Nobody really notices kids, and we will tell them in no uncertain terms to be really careful," explained Eddie.

"You're probably right, as much as I hate to admit it," said Mary Helen. "Have you two eaten? I was sort of waiting for you. The kids are in the dining room already. I'm sure they will be happy to hear this news."

The three kids broke into grins when the three adults came in.

"Have you got a secret assignment for us?" asked Lizzie, while Stephen and Maggie sat on the edge of their seats in anticipation. "And where is your disguise, Uncle Eddie?"

"Well, top of the morning to you too," said Eddie as the three adults took seats. "I figured it wasn't doing me any good, and besides, it was itching."

"I wouldn't have phrased it like that," said An Li. "But, yes, I guess we do have an assignment for you."

"What this comes down to is that you three are the only ones for the job," said Eddie. "We need you to keep watch on the Wild Horse, but if J.T., Braxton or Powell leave, we need you to follow."

"Get out of town," cried Stephen.

"This is not a game," blurted Mary Helen. "Those are three of the meanest men in this town."

"We know it's serious," said Maggie. "We just talk a little different."

"I can't help you," said Mary Helen. "I'm too well-known around town. I only agreed to this plan because Eddie and An Li have promised to give you a class in following someone."

"Sounds good," said Maggie. "We are taking it seriously, Mary Helen -- we really are."

"The first rule is my rule," said Mary Helen. "Do not split up or lose sight of each other, ever!"

"We all agreed, so we're counting on your word," said An Li.

"You have it," said Maggie, as Stephen and Lizzie nodded their heads.

"Okay. Listen up," said Eddie. "You always assume that the pigeon you are following is looking for a tail. That means you can't follow him around a blind turn. One way to avoid this is by being across the street and maybe a little ahead. People who think they are being followed typically just look behind them. John Bell, the current Chief, is one of the best at tailing someone. He always tells the young operatives to never let the pigeon get a good look at you. Always look around someone keeping most of yourself covered."

"That applies even if you are across the street," said An Li. "I think across the street will be the best strategy for you three to use when you can."

"That's what I did when I followed them before," said Stephen, quite proud of himself.

"The hardest thing will be if he gets on a trolley. One of you has to get on as far away from him as you can. I'm giving you plenty of money, so the other two should get a horse cab and try to beat the trolley to each stop. If you see the pigeon get off, stop the cabbie and go on foot again," instructed Eddie.

"Whoever is on the trolley should get off on the opposite side of the pigeon and try to keep him in view from the opposite side of the street again. You can walk singly or in a pair of girls or a girl and boy, but don't let him see all three of you together at the same time," continued An Li.

"Even though you're operating under the assumption that the pigeon is watching for a tail, if he starts making a series of turns or doubling back, get away from him. Get as far away as you can, but still try to keep him in sight, even if it's a couple of blocks," instructed Eddie. "I don't really know how to explain it, but once you are following somebody, you get like a rhythm going. It's like you are in sync with the pigeon. I think you will feel it as you go along. If you lose that feeling of being in sync, give him plenty of room."

"What do you want them to do if, Lord forbid, Powell or Braxton approaches them?" asked Mary Helen.

"I want you to scream your head off that this man touched you, if you know what I mean," said Eddie, blushing.

"We understand," said Maggie, looking at Lizzie.

"Same thing for me?" asked Stephen.

"Yes," answered An Li. "Once you start screaming, even those two will want to get away from you. People don't like other people mistreating children. They won't want to draw attention to themselves."

"All of you look at me," said Eddie. "This is an important case, but it is just "queer money"[5] in the end. It's not worth any of you, Mary Helen, An Li, or me getting hurt. You understand? If you think you are in the slightest bit of danger, leave it and get back here. We're going to get them. Time is on our side, agreed?"

Eddie stuck out his hand and each kid shook it.

"Okay," said Mary Helen. "While An Li and Eddie are leaving, we'll go and find you kids some different clothes."

"If I can, Mary Helen, I'd like to leave my bag here in case someone searches my room?" requested Eddie.

"Of course," she answered.

---

[5] ***Author's Note:*** *The term "queer" was common slang for counterfeit money around 1900. See newspaper article, Aspen, 1895, "Money Made by Women".*

"Here's some money," said An Li, giving each of them thirty dollars in varying denominations. "Don't worry about paying exact for the cab -- just overpay and get out."

"We'll do our best," promised Maggie.

"We know you will," answered Eddie, as he and An Li got up and headed out.

When they got to the lobby, Eddie said, "Why don't you give me ten minutes? That way if anybody is watching me, they won't put us together."

"Cool," said An Li, laughing, as he mimicked Stephen. "I'm going the opposite way. I'll meet you here tomorrow morning, unless I find out something important before then."

MONEY MADE BY WOMEN.

Females Who Vie with Men in Outwitting Uncle Sam.

Chief Hazen, the head of the Secret Service of the treasury department, is now in Canada, whither he has gone to extradite the noted woman counterfeiter, Mrs. Mack. There is no doubt that she will be convicted and sent to the penitentiary for her crimes.

Mrs. Mack is not the only woman who is under the arm of the law for this offense, for there are at least half a dozen more who have been caught "shoving the queer" during the past twelve months. Very few women make the bogus money, and almost the only part they play, as a rule, is to pass it. The men make the stuff and the women take it out to shop with, and thus get it into circulation. But if a woman is once suspected she is easily caught, because her sphere of action is so much more limited than that of a man. Anna Kelly of San Francisco is about the only woman, except Mrs. Farran, who makes the money herself. Her method is to imitate the coins of the country. This is done by having an alloy covered with silver, and by putting glass and a bit of copper into the composition, the weight and metallic ring of the genuine money are admirably imitated. All of the pictures of these women are in a huge case in the room of the Secret Service division. One woman so decidedly objected to having herself photographed that she was sketched while in court, and the pen-and-ink drawing is now preserved among the other photographs of the collection. As a rule, the women are rough in appearance and illiterate, and have hard countenances.

CHAPTER 30

Back in D.C., a Wells Fargo special messenger delivered a small package addressed to Jim Knox at the U.S. Secret Service Headquarters. While wearing cotton gloves, Knox quickly opened the package and removed the counterfeit coin. He put the coin on a tray and slid the tray under a large magnifying glass. He started making notes regarding various details of the counterfeit coin. Just as he was about to flip the coin, Chief Bell hurried in. It was obvious the all-knowing Doris had told him the package had arrived.

"So, what do you think, Jim?" asked the Chief.

"I think it's counterfeit," Knox said laughing. "Just a joke, Chief," he quickly added when Bell didn't crack a smile.

"It's really fine work. There are details or defects easily identified under the glass, but on the street, these are excellent. I haven't seen any counterfeits of this coin that I know of, but it just feels like work I've seen before. I'll weigh it and measure it and then I'll start reviewing counterfeit samples we have from the New York office. I wish I had more than just this one."

"Even if you can narrow it down to two or three cases, it would be a big help," answered the Chief. "Three men and a large woman, with one of the men being retarded, is a pretty unique group."

"There aren't that many counterfeit gold coins back East. The counterfeiters here seem to be moving toward paper money, so I'm hopeful. I'll be up as soon as I find anything. I don't care if it takes all night," said Knox.

"Thanks, Jim," said Bell. "I'll come down after hours and keep you company for awhile at least."

CHAPTER 31

Eddie again took a circuitous route back to his hotel. He got his usual three sets of newspapers and sat in the front parlor reading. He constantly scanned the street, but there was nobody he could see watching. Eddie was not a wait and see kind of guy. He noticed an ad in one of the newspapers for a boxing club, run by what appeared to be an Irishman. Eddie would have preferred to work out with An Li since the Kung Fu moves and exercises let him clear his mind. But today, boxing would have to do. He wasn't going anywhere near the Chinese section of town. Eddie left the hotel and went straight to the boxing club.

"Top of the morning," said Eddie to a short man sitting on a stool reading the paper.

"Aye, top of the morn yourself," he answered. "You a boxer, lad?"

"Only an amateur, but it's always a good idea to be prepared," answered Eddie, "especially in this town."

"I charge a dollar for non-members to come in. That includes all your togs and gloves. We don't do no bare knuckle stuff here," said the man.

"I'm Eddie Donnally, by the way," said Eddie.

"Most people call me Lefty," said the older man, shaking Eddie's hand.

Eddie changed into gym clothes, and for the next hour, Lefty worked him hard on the heavy bag and speed bag. Lefty gave him some tips on placing his feet properly, and Eddie complied. Eddie knew what he was doing but did a few things he knew Lefty would correct.

"You're pretty good lad," said Lefty.

"I have a cousin who runs a boxing club back in New York," answered Eddie. "I don't get in as much as I used to due to business."

"I figured you for one of those back East syndicate guys," laughed Lefty. "Since we're the only ones here, you want to spar a few rounds with an old man?"

"Sure," said Eddie. "But even money says you were a professional. I don't want to leave here looking like I've been in a brawl."

"Bad for business," laughed Lefty. "And, since you're a fellow Irishman, we'll just go easy."

Fifteen minutes later, Eddie was dripping with sweat, as was Lefty. Both men had traded blows, but the punches were not full out, a fact Eddie was glad of, since, despite his age, Lefty was outstanding.

"I'm calling uncle," said Eddie.

"Me too, lad. I enjoyed it. A lot of the guys that come in try to kill each other while sparring instead of improving their form and technique," replied Lefty. "There are showers in the back. Meet me in the office when you're ready and we'll have a little toast."

After Eddie showered and dressed, he went into Lefty's office and they shared a dram of single malt Irish whisky.

"This really is the good stuff," complimented Eddie.

"Me da always said, drink the best or nothing at all," replied Lefty.

"Good advice. I'm sure you'll see me again," said Eddie. "Thanks a lot."

"Come around anytime, laddie. I don't get many fellas in during the middle of the day, so that would be the best time," said Lefty.

Eddie strolled out of the boxing club and headed for the town library. He didn't try to check for a tail. He was going to bore anybody following him to death. Eddie spent the next several hours in the library. He had always been a voracious reader. He read all the Eastern newspapers and then skimmed a few books regarding the history of the Cripple Creek Mining District. Ultimately, he headed back to his hotel where he had a leisurely supper and then headed up to his room to wait for An Li's arrival.

While Eddie was busy trying to bore anyone tailing him, the kids were excited and keeping a close watch on the Wild Horse. A little after 11:00 a.m., Powell came out carrying a carpet bag satchel. Stephen got on the opposite side of the street and stayed out front of Powell. He walked on the inside of the sidewalk away from the street, and stayed behind other people as much as he could. Lizzie and Maggie were a half block behind Powell, and they kept him in view by peeking around other pedestrians. Powell went straight to the Victor short train terminal. All three kids saw him purchase a ticket to Victor. As soon as Powell moved down the platform, the trio relocated out of his sight.

"What do we do?" asked Lizzie. "Nobody said anything about this."

"I say we get in the last car and keep watching," said Stephen, looking at Maggie.

"I am with you. I think that this might be important," said

Maggie. "I'll go get three tickets."

The trio moved to the opposite end of the platform and were able to slip into the last car before it pulled out of the station.

"What do you want to do when we get to Victor?" asked Stephen.

"I'll go first and follow him from behind. You guys get off together and follow him on the other side of the street," said Maggie. "It's going to be crowded on the platform, so that's good."

It was only thirty minutes or so to Victor, and as Maggie had predicted, the platform was crowded. She shot off the train and hurried through the station to the street. There was no hurry. Powell just strolled down the street nice and easy. Maggie had no problems following him on the same side of the street, and she caught sight of Stephen and Lizzie a block and a half ahead of him on the opposite side. Five city blocks later, he turned into a garish saloon called the Golden Nugget. Stephen and Lizzie doubled back and came across the street when they saw Maggie had stopped.

"So, where did he go?" asked Lizzie.

"He went into the Golden Nugget over there," said Maggie.

"Let's look around for a place to watch the door, and maybe we can see if he comes out with that bag," said Stephen.

The words were barely out of Stephen's mouth when Powell strolled out the front door of the saloon.

"Look," said Lizzie excitedly. "No bag."

"You think we should keep following him, Mags?" asked Stephen.

"I don't think so. I think we need to go back to Haven House and hang out until we hear from Eddie," said Maggie.

"That probably won't be until tomorrow morning though,"

grumbled Stephen.

"I know. But I think this is important, and I'm sure he hasn't noticed us. We have nothing to gain but a lot to lose if he spots us now," replied Maggie.

CHAPTER 32

Miss Mildred's girl, Helene, had reported back to Tom where Eddie had gone that morning. "He stayed in there a pretty good while," said Helene. "And I saw a Chinaman come in also. Plus, the Eddie guy shaved off that beard"

"Good work," said Tom. "I'll have another crew get on him. Where is he now?"

"He's at that boxing gym down off Spencer Street," said Helene.

"You do good work girl," grinned Tom, giving her a five dollar gold piece.

"I'll be at the hotel early tomorrow," replied Helene.

Eddie had succeeded with his "boring day" and in the early evening, Tom sent all the girls home, back to Miss Mildred's. He rode out to the claim where Kira was waiting on the porch.

"So, what did you find out?" she demanded.

"The girls did a really good job, especially that Helene. He went to that goody-two shoes Haven House first thing in the morning and stayed awhile. Guess who she also saw going in?" asked Tom.

"A Chinaman?" growled Kira.

"Exactly," answered Tom. "I didn't try to follow him. Even the girls would be noticed in Chinatown."

"What else did that rat Donnally do?" asked Kira.

"Nothing. He went to that boxing gym for awhile. Then he just kind of wandered around and ended up at the library," answered Tom. "He may be a rat, but he is a boring one if today is any indication."

"He may be waiting for some of his stinking pals. Just keep following him until I'm ready," Kira said with a sneer.

"You sure you don't want to talk to J.T.?" asked Al.

Kira slapped her hand on the table. "No. Donnally is mine."

The brothers had never seen their sister look so menacing.

In their room, Al looked at Tom, Jr. "What'd you want me to do Al?" asked Tom. "I can't tell J.T. You saw how she is. I agree with you, but we'll just have to wait until she cools down a little and then we can convince her to use Braxton and Powell."

"Okay," said Al. "But I don't like this."

"Me either," answered Tom, blowing out the light.

CHAPTER 33

The next morning as Eddie was getting ready and Miss Mildred's girls were getting in place, in D.C., Jim Knox was rubbing his hands together and stretching. He had been in his vault all night. And now he thought he had an answer for the Chief, so he picked up the internal phone.

"Morning, Doris," he said.

"Morning to you, Jim. A little bird told me you have been here all night."

"Why am I not surprised?" laughed Jim.

"The Chief is here," said Doris. "You want to talk to him or do you want him to come down?"

"Ask him to come down, and you can come down yourself," replied Jim.

"Well, I believe I will, you sweet-talking devil," replied Doris before hanging up.

Five minutes later, the Chief and Doris came into the vault. Doris handed Jim a cup of coffee.

"Thanks," Jim said, with a big smile.

"Gee whiz, Jim. I didn't expect you to be here all night," said Chief Bell, who had left around eight the previous evening.

"Well, I knew I had seen some money similar to this. I wasn't giving up until I found it. This is too important," answered Knox. "Unfortunately, it's not a dead match, but I'm sure. You remember Tom Cassidy and his family up in New

York?"

"Who can forget," said the Chief. "But, he's been in jail maybe a couple of years, and if my memory serves me right, he pulled eight."

"You're right," answered Jim. "These coins are being struck from some of his molds and planchetts or someone he trained. Whoever it is, they are damn good. Excuse me, Doris," he added blushing.

Doris could barely contain a smile.

"There's no doubt in my mind that it's some of his family then. They hardly do anything except with family," said the Chief.

"I reviewed the records we have here and there's just not much about the family. The guys in New York are probably familiar with that whole bunch though," answered Knox.

"Doris, could you send a telegram to A.T. McCall and tell him we need any and all information they can come up with on Tom Cassidy and his family tree? Also, include that description we got from Eddie. Maybe it will speed things up," instructed the Chief. "I wish I could go to New York tomorrow. You know, to see how things are going at the office. But, unfortunately, I'm stuck here."

He got no reply from Knox and Doris, just raised eyebrows.

Within the hour, A.T. McCall had the Chief's telegram and was headed out to hit up some snitches about Tom Cassidy. He wasn't planning on visiting many Irish bars, since he was looking for personal information, and the bar snitches were notoriously tight-lipped on personal information.

A.T. caught an uptown subway train and started reflecting on the upcoming weekend. A.T. McCall was an Irishman with bright red hair and fair skin. As much as Eddie was not your typical Irishman in the looks category, A.T. could be nothing else. There was one exception - he was big, 6'3" and 200 lbs. of muscle. He liked to box and wrestle, but usually his opponents were done after one session,. A.T. was also smart. He had gone to law school like An Li for a year, but that was enough. It was way too boring. He had gone to his Uncle, a New York precinct captain, about joining the NYC Police Department. His Uncle had looked up at him and said, "Son, you are too smart for the police department. The Chief of the Secret Service is coming to town next week and I want you to meet him. It hadn't taken Chief Taylor ten minutes to recruit A.T. The next morning, the Chief swore him in at the New York Office and issued him a badge and a gun. A.T. was an eager learner and all the "old hands" looked after the kid.

A.T. was single and had his own apartment, but his mother was after him to get married. The thought made A.T. smile to himself. There was going to be hell-to-pay. A.T. was a regular church-goer and had met an Italian girl, Lucia, at the church. He had been taking her out for six months, and they both knew they were meant for each other. Lucia's parents knew A.T. and were no problem. A.T. didn't think his parents would be a problem. They were born in America, but his grandma, who was one-hundred percent Irish, would throw a fit. They will get over it A.T. thought. At least she's Catholic. He and Lucia had decided to go to Sunday dinner this week at his parent's. He could hardly wait.

A.T. got off the train in a not quite middle-class neighborhood. It was a hodge-podge of businesses and residences mixed together. Most stores were on street level, and the shop owners and their families lived above. McCall could smell corn beef and cabbage cooking somewhere. Gotta love us

Irish he thought.   His destination was a grocery store just outside the neighborhood where Tom Cassidy lived before his incarceration.   A.T. bought a newspaper from a street vendor and eyed the people on the street. He didn't expect to see any known criminals in this area, but he wanted to be as sure as he could be. This guy was a good source, and it wouldn't do for someone to spot a Secret Service Operative going into his shop. After a few minutes, A.T. was satisfied, so he stepped into the store.

"Morning, Jimmy," said A.T. "How's business?"

Jimmy twitched as he stuttered, "Good, good."

A.T. knew Jimmy was running a penny-ante numbers racket out of his store. In exchange for information, A.T. and the other New York operatives were keeping it quiet.   Jimmy was a wealth of information and nobody suspected him of working with the Service.

"Let's step into my office," said Jimmy, nervously.

"Margaret, just leave that stocking and work the register, please," said Jimmy to a young woman stocking shelves.

Once in his back office, Jimmy sat down and looked expectantly up at A.T.

"I need a little background info," said A.T., taking another office chair.   "You remember Tom Cassidy, the coin counterfeiter?"

"Sure," said Jimmy. "I think almost everyone in Irish town knows that family. It was rumored around town that you guys didn't get all his dies and molds, but nobody seems to know where they are."

"It would be nice to know that, but I'm looking for info about his family. I know about his brothers. Did he have any kids?"

"Not really," said Jimmy. "But, he and his wife took in his sister's brood several years ago before his wife died."

"Why did they to that?" asked A.T.

"Word was that his brother-in-law got killed in a mining accident out West," answered Jimmy.

A.T. tried to hide his excitement. "So, tell me a little about them," he replied, pulling out a small journal.

"They used to come in here sometimes. There were four of them, three boys and a girl. One of the boys was named Tom, but everyone used to call him Junior. After big Tom went to prison, most people stopped calling him Junior. Then there was Al and Nate. Al was just a regular kid, but Nate was a retard. He could get around okay, but he followed his sister around most of the time. Her name is Kira, and she is a rough one. One day one of the boys from down the block made fun of Nate and that girl almost beat him to death. It took two grown men to pull her off. She's crazy that one."

"What does she look like, exactly?" asked A.T.

"She's not a pretty one," said Jimmy. "She's big and built kind of square. She talks like a woman, but I swear she's the meanest woman in Irish town."

"She ever get in any trouble?" asked A.T.

"Not that I ever heard of, but everybody said she worshipped her Uncle Tom. At his trial, she was there every day. A lot of people thought she got all of Tom's stuff and that he taught her everything he knew."

"Have you seen her or the brothers around lately?" asked A.T.

"No. They disappeared quite awhile back, right after the trial, and nobody seems to know where they went," answered Jimmy. A.T. asked some more general questions which Jimmy gladly answered.

"Okay," said A.T., rising. "Thanks. I owe you one."

"Is that all?" asked Jimmy, somewhat relieved. "I can get you that kind of stuff anytime, Mr. McCall."

"I'm sure I'll be back," said A.T., leaving the man's office. "Oh, by the way, what last name do they have?"

"They all go by Cassidy," said Jimmy quickly, glad to be rid of A.T. McCall.

A.T. didn't even bother going back to the Field Office. He grabbed a horse cab to Grand Central Station and then caught the next express train to D.C., but not before sending Lucia a telegram letting her know where he was going and promising to be back soonest.

CHAPTER 34

The next morning, even though he was pre-occupied with going to Haven House, Eddie still took a round-about route getting there. But Tom had done what Kira had instructed. He had four new girls, although he had kept Helene. Helene was actually smarter than Tom, and had suggested she take up a position to watch the front of Haven House. Helene's suggestion was not just smart; she had an ulterior motive. She had heard about Haven House and its' mission. Helene, unknown to many, was an educated woman. She had come West with her new husband intending to teach school. Unfortunately, her choice of a husband had been a mistake. He had caught the gold fever, and nothing would do him but to go to Cripple Creek. Helene had hoped to teach school, but they were barely settled when her husband started frequenting the gambling halls. Within a week, he was shot dead in a cheating dispute. Helene was penniless, alone and desperate. So, she had ended up with Miss Mildred.

Miss Mildred may have been a Madam, and not formally educated, but she was smart. She spoke often with Helene, and only referred the best gentlemen to her. Helene started keeping the books and managing the business aspect of the house. In exchange, Mildred referred fewer and fewer gentlemen, until it stopped altogether. Helene wished Haven House had been there when she needed it. Unlike most of the Meyers Avenue residents, Helene admired Mary Helen McDougal and the work she did. Helene was snapped out of her reverie by the sight of An Li stepping off a trolley and entering Haven House. It wasn't fifteen minutes until she saw Eddie Donnally glide around the corner, obviously checking to make sure no one followed. Helene wondered, not for the first time, why Tom Cassidy wanted this guy followed. It was costing him a whole lot of money, so it had to be important.

"Top of the morning, everyone," exclaimed Eddie, as he found Mary Helen, An Li and the kids at a table in the staff dining room.

Just as Eddie sat down, Miss Ellie appeared at the table. "Would you care for the usual, Mr. Donnally?" she asked.

"Yes, ma'am," he replied jovially. "Without, please."

"We'll see," Miss Ellie replied, walking away.

Eddie turned to the others and started. "Jeez, you kids look like you're about to explode."

Eddie looked at An Li, who shrugged, and then at Mary Helen.

Mary Helen said, "It's their story. I'll let them tell it."

"I'll start," blurted Stephen.

"Okay," said Eddie. "But, it's more polite to let ladies go first."

"It's alright," said Maggie, knowingly. "We'll correct anything he gets wrong."

So, that's what they did. When they were done, Eddie and An Li smiled broadly.

"You three are something," said An Li, who was making notes in a pocket journal.

"This guy, Powell, didn't even try to see if he was being followed?" queried Eddie.

"If he did, he is terrible at it," answered Maggie. "We were very careful, but he didn't look behind him even once."

Rising, Mary Helen said, "I've got some work to do in my office. I'll leave you to yours."

"You guys go over the details with An Li," instructed Eddie. "I'd like to speak with Mary Helen in her office."

An Li and the kids stared at Eddie as he followed Mary Helen out of the dining room. Eddie glanced back and colored slightly when he saw the stares.

"What's up with that?" Stephen asked An Li. "We already told you everything. There are no more details."

An Li raised one eyebrow, and the girls stared.

"Get out-of-town!" exclaimed Stephen. "Really?"

"I've known Eddie a long time. He enjoys the company of women, but usually not the same woman. There definitely seems to be some chemistry between those two," related An Li.

"Whatever," replied Stephen, somewhat disappointed in Eddie.

"An Li, would it be alright if we came to Chinatown for lunch?" asked Lizzie.

"We love Chinese food," said Maggie.

"I think that would be an excellent idea. I think you guys have been around the Wild Horse enough for a little while. You should take the Main Street and Union trolley. Get off at Stop #7 and turn left. About three blocks down, you'll see a Chinese Pharmacy. I'll meet you there at say 12:30."

"Sounds great," said Stephen.

"Fine," said An Li. "I know you told us everything, but just let me ask you a few more questions about yesterday."

Mary Helen moved behind her desk as Eddie shut the door. After they both sat down, she looked at him curiously.

"I was hoping you would allow me to escort you to dinner this evening," said Eddie.

Mary Helen stared for just a second and said, "Are you asking me out, Mr. Donnally, or is this part of your case?"

Eddie colored slightly and said, "I came to ask you out, but if it wouldn't offend you, maybe we could go to Victor and I could get a look at this Golden Nugget."

"That would be fine. I like killing two birds with one stone. Although after the other night, maybe we should skip the killing part," she answered with a smile.

"I really was going to suggest we go to Victor, anyway," said Eddie. "There's less chance of anyone there noticing us together."

"I can be ready by seven," said Mary Helen. "I do have a responsibility here, you know."

"I know," answered Eddie, rising. "I better get back to An Li and work out some strategy."

"Would you send the kids in to fill me in when you are done?" she asked.

"Yes, ma'am," said Eddie, going out the door. Once out in the hall, Eddie's face broke into a grin, and he hurried back to the dining room.

An Li was just finishing up his notes. "The kids are coming to Chinatown for lunch," said An Li. "I think they have been around the Wild Horse enough for awhile and could use a day off."

"Good plan," said Eddie. "I'll check out the Golden Nugget tonight. I'm expecting to get a telegram from Washington that might help us." He turned to face the children. "Mary Helen wanted you to come tell her what you will be up to today."

"Okay," said Maggie. "So, we'll meet again in the morning?"

"As long as Mary Helen will have us," answered Eddie as the kids left the dining room.

An Li asked, "You want me to get in disguise and cover you in Victor?"

"I think it's a good idea. I asked Mary Helen to dinner in Victor so I could see the layout," said Eddie.

An Li stared. "You just had to take Mary Helen with you for a cover, I suppose."

"Don't give me that look!" exclaimed Eddie.

"The last time I saw you acting like this was, what, twenty years ago. We were in the eighth grade, and you had a crush on what's her name," laughed An Li.

"Shut up," said Eddie. "What is it your grandfather says? Oh, yeah, Confucius say man who talks too much gets a sore jaw!"

"What time?" asked An Li, still smirking.

"I'm picking Mary Helen up at 7:00 p.m.," answered Eddie.

"My inscrutable self will observe you in Victor," answered An Li, with a twinkle in his eyes.

Eddie just shook his head as he got up and left the dining room.

An Li stayed another ten minutes going over his notes before leaving himself.

Helene saw Eddie come out and told Emmy, the girl browsing with her in the store, to get going. "Give him plenty of room," instructed Helene. "I'll get the next trolley."

Helene caught the next trolley, and as the car was pulling off, she saw An Li coming out of the Haven House.

Maggie, Stephen and Lizzie got to the Chinese Pharmacy at 12:30 sharp. An Li was standing outside talking to several Chinese businessmen. The men moved on as the kids walked up.

"Is it a little weird that we are the only non-Chinese people anywhere?" asked Stephen.

"It is Chinatown," said Lizzie.

"Diversity is not a real common theme around here," said Maggie.

"Welcome to Chinatown," said An Li. "Come inside and meet Grandfather Chung."

The trio was amazed at all the herbs and various items within the pharmacy. All were in different sized jars covered with Chinese characters. They entered a room that was light and airy with several work tables.

"Grandfather, please meet my friends, Maggie, Stephen and Lizzie," said An Li. He had tried to tell Chung about the leprechaun and the kids, but the words wouldn't come out. So, he settled for telling Chung that they were relatives of Eddie's who were in town giving them a hand. It had sounded lame even to him, but Chung had just smiled.

The older man came around and gave a slight bow to the three kids. "Any friend of An Li's is worthy of being called family," he said.

"Thank you," said Lizzie. "We are honored grandfather."

The old man smiled as Stephen and Maggie gaped at Lizzie's politeness. They quickly recovered and greeted Chung.

"I understand you like Chinese food," stated Chung.

"We do," answered Maggie, "although, what we are used to may not be as authentic as what is served here."

"Don't worry," said Chung. "An Li and I will guide you."

The group went out the side door and over several streets to a restaurant.

"Dude, that smells good!" exclaimed Stephen, as they got close.

An Li just shook his head.

As the group entered the restaurant, conversation all but stopped. Chung said in a loud voice," Everyone, these are my friends, Maggie, Stephen and Lizzie. I would appreciate you granting them all the courtesy you would give my family."

Many in the small room applauded, and several at the closest tables stood up and bowed to the trio. The children politely bowed back.

"Wow," said Stephen.

"Thank you, grandfather," said Maggie. "You obviously are very revered around here."

"That often comes with age," laughed Chung. "Have a seat."

"What is your favorite dish?" asked An Li. "Many people in New York like fried rice."

"That's my favorite," said Lizzie, "especially with chicken."

An Li said a few words in Chinese to the waitress who smiled and headed for the kitchen.

"Do you have Szechwan here?" asked Stephen.

"Of course," answered An Li. "They have an excellent dish made with noodles. I'll tell her when she comes back. I have had it several times. What about you, Maggie?"

"I like both," she answered.

Over the next hour, it was a veritable feast. "This is as good as anything back home," said Stephen.

"I'm glad you enjoyed it," said Chung, with a big smile. "Unfortunately, we don't get many outsiders here."

"They don't know what they're missing," said Stephen, sitting back with a sigh.

"Now that we are quite finished, let's go back to the pharmacy," suggested Chung.

Once back at the pharmacy, they all pulled up stools. "I'm

glad you wanted to come here," said An Li. "You are now under the protection of the entire Chinese community."

"What does that mean exactly?" asked Maggie.

"I see you are the practical one," said Chung. "It means that if you are in any trouble, tell any Chinese person in town that I am your grandfather and show them this." Chung handed each of them a Chinese medallion bearing a dragon on one side and a Chinese character on the other. "They will help you."

"Cool," said Stephen.

"Okay, enough," said An Li. "I have work to do. You three need to go back to Haven House and see if you can give Mary Helen a hand this afternoon."

The trio said their good-byes and left the pharmacy headed for the trolley stop.

An Li said," Grandfather, I will be going out and covering my partner in Victor tonight."

"Ah," said Chung. "Good luck. Do be careful. Our people are still looking out for the three men and the woman."

"I have faith it will happen," said An Li, rising to leave.

CHAPTER 35

Helene went back to Miss Mildred's and worked on the books. At five, she left and met Tom and Al at a small saloon off the beaten path. As soon as she sat, Tom said, "This rat is one boring guy. All he seems to do is read papers and wander around town."

"Why is this guy so interesting to you?" asked Helene.

"His name is Eddie Donnally, and he's the Secret Service Operative that put our Uncle Tom in prison for eight years," explained Tom, with the intention of impressing Helene.

"Does Mildred know who he is?" asked Helene.

"No," answered Al, "and big mouth here shouldn't have told you either. Kira would throw a fit if she knew."

"You won't say anything, will you Helene?" asked Tom, giving her a $20 gold double eagle.

"No. I'll keep your secret," answered Helene. "I never knew how you guys came up with your money," she continued questioningly.

"No more secrets," barked Al at Tom. "That would be none of your business, missy."

"Okay, okay," said Helene. "They keep going to that Haven House and I'm thinking the only way to learn more is from the inside."

"What did you have in mind?" asked Tom.

"I could go there and tell them a sad story and see if they

would take me in," Helene answered.

"I don't know," said Al. "Maybe we should ask Kira."

"No," bellowed Tom.   "Not with the mood she's been in. I'm tired of her yelling just because that rat is not doing anything. I hear that the woman running the place is Irish and a real looker. You think he's sweet on her?"

"I don't know," answered Helene, "but you boys double my fee and I'm in."

"Deal," said Tom, shaking Helene's hand and holding on to it a few seconds longer. "When this is over, maybe me and you can do some real business."

Helene smiled. "That sounds pretty good."

Helene rose, waved good-bye to the two brothers, and walked out of the saloon, conscious that Al and Tom were admiring her every step.   When Helene got outside, she shuddered. There's not enough gold in Cripple Creek to let that jerk paw me she thought. She was thinking about what Tom had told her as she walked.

So, Eddie Donnally was Secret Service.   That means the Cassidys are counterfeiters and he's on their trail. Helene had heard of Secret Service Operatives and their reputation. Eddie Donnally and that Chinaman were not regular lawmen. Anyway, I want to get out of Mildred's and this is a way of getting into Haven House, she thought. It wasn't quite dark, so she decided to go to the Haven House and see how hard it was to get in.

As Helene got off the trolley and got in sight of Haven House, she stopped and stared.   Eddie Donnally and she guessed that Mary Helen lady were coming out, and both were dressed up. Well, let's see where this goes, she thought, as she started to follow them.

CHAPTER 36

Eddie and Mary Helen caught the short train line that went to Victor.

"I'm glad you said yes," Eddie told her.

"Well, we Irish have to stick together," she replied with a twinkle in her eye.

They spent the relatively short ride talking about New York and things they had in common from the City. As they exited the trolley and started walking toward the restaurant, Mary Helen put her arm through Eddie's. Eddie wouldn't have noticed if an elephant was following him. He was too caught up in the moment.

Helene was watching a block back. These two are sweet on each other. She thought wistfully about her dead husband and her life before Miss Mildred's. She would get into Haven House, but there was no way she would tell Tom much of anything. When the time is right, I might just have a talk with Mr. Eddie Donnally, Secret Service Operative!

"So, what do you really think of Cripple Creek?" asked Mary Helen.

"I think it's probably the way New York was a few years ago when so many immigrants were coming into the city. Everyone was hustling about trying to make a better life for themselves and their families," answered Eddie. "Actually, parts of New York are still like that as more immigrants keep coming in."

"I would agree," said Mary Helen, "but mining is really hard. Most of these miners will be dead before they are 30 or 35."

"That's a depressing thought," said Eddie.

"It is," said Mary Helen. "So, tell me the stories of some of your cases. Aunt Lucy told me you are quite the operative."

Over dinner, Eddie told her the story of Pinky McFadden, Will Scott, Miguel and several cases he and An Li had worked. Mary Helen was entranced by the easy way Eddie told the stories. He wasn't bragging or boasting, just telling the tales as they were. He really is something, she thought. Most men would be bragging and trying to impress her.

"Coffee or dessert, sir?" asked their server breaking the spell.

"I'll have coffee. What about you, Mary Helen?" asked Eddie.

"Coffee will be fine," she answered.

"We've almost wore out our welcome. There's hardly anybody left in here," said Eddie.

Neither had noticed most of the customers leaving. They had their coffees and then left to take a walk by the Golden Nugget. The joint was hopping Eddie noted. It had pretty much the same games as the Wild Horse.

"I wish I could watch you work these crooked games," said Mary Helen, wistfully.

"I'd love to take you with me, but your reputation would never be the same," answered Eddie laughing. "I'll bring some cards over in the morning and show you some tricks."

"As Stephen would say, 'cool'," laughed Mary Helen.

"Those kids sure do talk funny, don't they?" Eddie responded.

An Li, in his disguise, had been walking the streets around the restaurant. He sat down frequently, acting the old man. He was beginning to think they were never coming out. When they did, his jaw dropped as he saw their entwined arms and eyes for nothing but each other. He thought he had spotted a woman following, but he dismissed her when she kept walking and never appeared again.

Gansulk had it easy this night. He found a place in the shadows and could have put an arrow in anyone trying to hurt An Li or Eddie without ever moving. An Li paralleled Eddie and Mary Helen's stroll by the Golden Nugget with Gansulk ever in the shadows.

Eddie and Mary Helen caught the short train back to Cripple Creek. An Li walked around mulling things over until the next train. He then made his way back to Chinatown, never noticing the small Mongolian in his wake.

CHAPTER 37

A T. McCall got to Chief Bell's office in the late afternoon. His train had been delayed, which was not an unusual occurrence.

"Afternoon, Doris," he said, surprising her.

"Hey, A.T.," she said. "This is a pleasant surprise."

"I've got the info the Chief was looking for, so I hot-footed it down here," he answered. "Maybe we could grab some supper after we wrap things up here. I bet I could even get Jim to go with us."

"Why, A.T., you sure know how to impress a girl," said Doris smiling. "You go on in. The Chief is practically pacing the floor. Tell him I'm calling down to Jim to get him up here too."

A.T. tapped on the Chief's door and went in. Doris was right. The Chief was pacing the floor deep in thought.

"Afternoon Chief," said A.T.

The Chief started and then his face broke into a grin. "Outstanding. I take it you have made some real progress and are not just here to fix Jim up with Doris?"

A.T.'s mouth dropped open. "You know about that?" he asked.

"That's why I'm the Chief, son," he responded, still grinning.

That elicited a chuckle from A.T. "I'm almost positive I know who we are looking for, Chief. Doris sent for Jim Knox, and I'm about to make him doubly happy."

As if on cue, Jim Knox burst through the door panting. "Sorry Chief, but I ran up the steps. Afternoon, A.T.," he replied, extending a handshake.

"Okay A.T., let's hear it," ordered the Chief.

"After your telegram, I went to see one of my main Irish snitches. He runs a grocery store on the outskirts of a big Irish area. He runs a small numbers racket, and we let him slide since he is very helpful on occasion. He was extremely cooperative since I was just looking for background information. He told me that Tom Cassidy had four kids come live with him several years ago. It seems their father was killed in a mining accident in Colorado and the wife pawned them off to the family. The three boys are Tom, Al and Nate. The girl is Kira. Nate is retarded. Rumor is that it was a hard delivery without a doctor anywhere around. Tom and Al are just followers, but Kira, the leader, is the tough one. It seems she was Tom Cassidy's favorite. Word is that he taught her everything he knew about counterfeiting gold coins. She was at his trial every day, so she at least would recognize Eddie. We never recovered all of Tom's equipment, and my snout[6] says she would be the one to know where it was hidden.

He also says no one has seen any of them in many months; and rumor is, the girl left town with probably at least some, if not all, of Tom's equipment right after the trial. My snout says word on the street is she is damn good and certain people have tried to find her for business purposes, with no success."

"That makes a lot of sense," said Jim Knox. "I looked at all the coins we know came from Tom, and there are some variations among them. But, they are all real good. I also

---

[6] ***Author's Note:*** *Snout is archaic slang for confidential informant.*

examined others that we are unsure of. After what you just told me, I think this Kira probably at least did the engraving work, if not the whole process, on the coin from Colorado."

"Did you have any arrest or suspect cards with photos?" asked the Chief.

"No," said A.T. "Tom was always the focus. We didn't really even know about the girl and her brothers. My snout says the girl is a really tough one, and her description matches the one Eddie sent. He also told me that she was ranting and raving about Eddie after Tom got sentenced to eight years in the pen."

"Excellent work, A.T.," praised the Chief. "Your snout was quite the fountain of information."

"Yeah, he's always good for information and background on other people. He's a little more skittish about telling on actual operations," answered A.T.

"I think it's a reasonable conclusion that she and the brothers are the ones doing the counterfeiting," said Jim Knox. "She definitely would also have the skill and touch to drill the bars."

"She obviously has others besides her brothers involved, and I think Eddie and An Li have identified some of them," said the Chief. "Hopefully, with the names, they will be able to track her down."

"I asked the snout, and he said the girl is mean enough and hates Eddie enough to kill him," offered A.T. "The only thing is, she looks after the retarded brother like a mother hen. She will probably stay in the background, even though she would personally like to kill Eddie herself. She is sure tough enough. The snout said some guys were making fun of Nate and Kira went nuts. She had one guy down on the ground and it took two grown men to pull her off him."

"Okay," said the Chief. "I'll code a message to Eddie and get it off right away."

"I got a little better description of all of them from the snout," said A.T., handing the Chief four suspect cards. "You want me to head out there, Chief?" he asked.

"Eddie hasn't asked for any more operatives. I think An Li has some strong contacts within the Chinese community that they are enlisting for help. So, not right now, but that's not to say we might not need you in the near future," answered the Chief. "You two beat it so I can code this message," ordered the Chief. "And, A.T., you can tell Doris she can leave early today," he replied with a grin and a wink.

After the two men left, the Chief got his thoughts together and began coding his message.

A.T. told Doris and Jim to meet him at Luigi's on Fourteenth Street at 8:00 p.m. for dinner and reserved a table for two. He clued the maitre de in and then headed to Union Station. The maitre de would say A.T. got called back to New York and they should go ahead without him. At 8 o'clock, A.T. was halfway back to New York and smiling to himself.

CHAPTER 38

Eddie and Mary Helen got off the short train and walked arm-in-arm down the street. Eddie was thinking he'd like to walk miles like this, but they arrived quickly at Haven House.

Turning toward Eddie, Mary Helen said, "I think that was the best evening I've had since coming to Cripple Creek thanks to you, Mr. Eddie Donnally."

"I can say the same, but I've only been here a few days," replied Eddie. He pulled her close and kissed her. To his delight, she kissed him right back, wrapping her arms around his neck. When they finally broke apart, Mary Helen said, "I would invite you in, but the kids."

'I know," said Eddie. "That's another reason I'm going to kick that little leprechaun's butt when I see him again."

Mary Helen laughed. "Good night, Eddie," and she went into Haven House.

Eddie thought about Mary Helen all the way back to his hotel. This is not good at all he thought. I've already been shot at, and what was he thinking when he asked Mary Helen out. Talk about stupid. As he entered the hotel, the pompous desk man raised his hand, "I have a telegram for you, Mr. Donnally."

"What time did it come?" asked Eddie.

"Shortly after you left, sir," said the shorter man, giving Eddie the envelope like it was a hot potato. Eddie took the stairs to his room two at a time laughing to himself. There was no doubt the wormy little clerk had looked at the telegram, which was just a jumble of letters and numbers. Once in his room, Eddie got out his wheel and opened the telegram. He laughed. This long a telegram must have cost the Chief $20.00. Eddie pored over the message for an hour before he finished. Outstanding, he thought. We've got a name; and now it all makes sense. I vaguely remember the young woman who was at that trial. Now all we have to do is smoke them out, he thought, while undressing and crawling into bed.

The next morning, the usual group convened for breakfast at the Haven House. Eddie passed around the telegram from the Chief, starting with An Li, of course.

The others crowded around him and read over his shoulder.

"This is great!" exclaimed Stephen.

It is, but why are Mary Helen and Eddie not looking so happy thought Maggie.

"I'll get these names to Grandfather Chung, and I predict we will have a location by tomorrow," beamed An Li.

"My plan is to go to Victor and teach a crooked gambler a lesson," said Eddie.

"Can we go with you?" asked Stephen.

"No, I really don't want anyone associating you guys with me," answered Eddie. "I'd like you to go back to watching the Wild Horse."

"Let's all meet back here at supper time," said Mary Helen. "I've got a new lady that checked in last night. I need to get her settled."

"Sounds good," said An Li. "Until this evening," he said, taking his leave.

The kids saw how Mary Helen and Eddie were looking at

each other and decided to leave them alone.

"We're going to change clothes before we head out," said Maggie as the three exited the room.

"I really enjoyed last night," said Eddie.

"Maybe we can do it again sometime," answered Mary Helen.

"You can count on it," replied Eddie.

"Now, get going Mr. Donnally, and teach those cheats a lesson," said Mary Helen, smiling.

CHAPTER 39

While Eddie and Mary Helen were out in Victor, a raging family argument was taking place among the Cassidys. Most of the raging was coming from Kira. Her rage at Eddie Donnally was all consuming. The steady, meticulous engraver was gone.

"I'll tell you what we are going to do," said Kira.

"C'mon, Kira. We know it's him and the Chinaman," said Tom.

"If you don't think they have identified us yet, then you're as stupid as Nate," she grumbled. "We are going to take care of Eddie stinking Donnally and his little band tomorrow."

"Maybe Tom's right, Kira," said Al. "Let's give it a little time. We've got one of Miss Mildred's girls inside that Haven House. We think Donnally is sweet on the Irish lady that runs the place."

"Shut up," snarled Kira. "I'm in charge here. If you don't like it, you can walk. But, all I have to do is talk to J.T. and Braxton and Powell will make you disappear."

Tom and Al just stared, and both knew she meant it. "Okay," said Tom. "We're with you. Just tell us your plan."

"That's my brothers talking," said Kira, smiling and getting the Irish whisky and glasses out.

"Tomorrow morning, I want you to get your girls outside the Haven House and then follow the Chinaman," she instructed.

"Al, you and another set of girls follow Donnally. Just keep back. Late in the afternoon, we are going to make our play. I'll bring the wagon into town with a tarp. We'll try to get the Chinaman first, then the woman, and then I'm going to get Donnally."

"Jeez," said Tom. "Are we going to kill all three? We don't even know for sure that Donnally is sweet on the woman."

"No. I'm going to kill all three," she snarled. "I'm going to kill his partner first right in front of him and then the woman. She must mean something to him if he keeps going there. And then I'm going to gut him with my knife just like a fish."

Tom and Al didn't say anything, just drank their whisky. There was nothing to say to a woman with an insane gleam in her eyes. Nate was hiding in his room. He didn't like all the commotion. It scared him.

While Eddie's group was in the Haven House the next morning, Tom and Al were following Kira's orders. As An Li came out, the girls started their tail with Al hanging way back. Tom and his girls did the same when Eddie came out. The girls were good, and one of them saw An Li go up the stairs to his office. She walked by and saw the lawyer's office sign tacked to the wall. She continued on to the pharmacy intending to use it as her excuse to be in Chinatown. When she entered the pharmacy, a bell tingled and an old man came out of the back.

"Good morning, madam," said Chung. "How can I help you?"

The girl had not expected a Chinaman that spoke perfect English.

"A friend told me she got medicine from you that helped her bad headaches," she stammered, trying not to act nervous.

"Of course," replied Chung. "I have a bottle of the headache potion right here." Chung walked over to the wall shelves and removed a small bottle. "If you put this potion in tea twice a day, your headaches will be no more," Chung said, bowing slightly.

"How much do I owe you?" asked the girl.

"For such a beautiful woman, it is, how you say, on the house," replied Chung smiling.

The girl left, and headed back to meet Al to tell him what she had found out about the Chinaman. She had visions of a big tip, and she got it.

As soon as the girl left, Chung called his wife. "I've just had a very unusual customer. I need Gansulk now please."

His wife rushed out the side door to fulfill his request. While she was out, the old man kept watch out his front window on the steps to An Li's office. Gansulk rushed in ten minutes later.

"What is the problem, grandfather?" he asked.

"I just had a very interesting visitor," replied Chung. "It was a white woman, and I know she was not what she appeared to be."

"Are we going to tell An Li?" asked Gansulk.

"No," said Chung. "He is doing very important work. We do need to watch him now constantly, though."

"That is not a problem," answered Gansulk. "My oldest son has been helping me just in case he was needed."

"Very wise," said Chung. "Very wise. I see An Li headed this way. I am leaving it in your hands."

"It is my honor," said Gansulk, as he headed out the back door.

"Greetings grandfather," said An Li, entering the pharmacy. "We have good news. The people we are looking for are named Cassidy. The woman's name is Kira, and the three men are her brothers, Tom, Al and Nate. Nate is the retarded one."

"I will spread the word immediately," said Chung. "This is a major development."

"Only if one of our people can identify the site where they are counterfeiting the bars and the money," replied An Li.

"Not to worry, my son," said Chung. "We should know by nightfall."

"I sure hope so," said An Li.

"We will have lunch together," stated Chung.

"Of course," said An Li. "Say about 1:00 o'clock?"

"Excellent," said Chung as An Li turned to leave.

Tom's girls were also doing well. It had been tricky, but they managed to follow Eddie to Victor. One of the girls saw him enter the Golden Nugget. She hurried back to the trolley terminal to let Tom know.

"The Golden Nugget! Are you sure?" he asked incredulously.

"Of course I'm sure," snapped the girl.

"I'm going back to Cripple Creek. You girls keep up the good work," he said, handing her a $5 gold piece.

Once inside the Golden Nugget, Eddie surveyed the tables. Even this early in the morning, the place was half-full with late shift miners. Eddie got a drink. Definitely too early to gamble, he thought, and began watching the tables.

While Eddie and An Li were going about their business, Mary Helen was going about hers. She was sitting on the sofa in her office facing Helene.

"How long have you been here?" asked Mary Helen.

"About five years," said Helene.

"Would you like to tell me what you have been doing for money?" asked Mary Helen soothingly.

"I'm sure you know," said Helene, blushing and looking down.

"People do what they have to do to survive, Helene," said Mary Helen, taking the other woman's hand. "There is no shame in that." Mary Helen thought Helene was beautiful. She was small and petite and had huge soulful eyes.

Helene began to cry, and over the next hour, she told Mary Helen her whole story. Five years of anguish and shame came rushing out. The only thing that shocked Mary Helen was the revelations about Eddie being followed.

"I'm so sorry," blurted Helene.

"Stop," said Mary Helen. "You've done the right thing. Eddie and his partner know about Tom and the whole family. It's just a matter of time before they are arrested."

"Do you know where they live?" asked Mary Helen.

"No," said Helene. "I know it's not in town, though."

"Come on," said Mary Helen. "We're going over to Doc Simpson's and let him give you a full check-up. Don't worry. I'll be with you the whole way. We do this for everyone we take in."

"Okay," said Helene. "I'm ready."

Eddie had lunch at the bar and then went to work. He hit several tables, winning a little and losing a little. Then he started working at the Faro table. He was soon on a winning streak and drawing a crowd to the table. A man in a brocade vest pushed his way through the crowd around the table. Eddie nodded to the man and thought to himself. This guy is J.T.'s brother. They weren't twins, but there was no mistaking the family resemblance.

Eddie said to the dealer, "How about hold my chips while I have a word with the boss?" The crowd around the table groaned, because many had been busy making side bets and winning. J.T.'s brother turned, and Eddie followed in his wake.

Once in his office, the man turned and glared at Eddie.

"I must apologize, sir. My name is Eddie Donnally, and you obviously are related to J.T. Raines," stated Eddie.

"How do you know my brother, J.T.?" asked the man suspiciously.

"He and I are in the process of forming a partnership in some business that I am not at liberty to discuss. J.T. can fill you in if he wants," smiled Eddie. "I didn't know this place belonged to J.T.'s brother."

"You are quite the card shark," said the man. "My name is Elwood, by the way."

"If you would collect my winnings, I will be glad to return them to you and take my business elsewhere," said Eddie. "Is there a competitor that you could recommend?"

"Oh, yeah," said Elwood grinning. "About three blocks down is the Silver Spur. They could use a good fleecing."

"Fine," said Eddie. "I can oblige."

Elwood stuck out his hand for Eddie to shake, and said, "You're a square guy. Listen, let me give you your money out of my stash back here," said Elwood.

Eddie looked at him questioningly.

"Let's just say the money out there is not as good as the money back here," said Elwood, giving Eddie a wink. He gave Eddie his money.

"Thanks," said Eddie. "I hadn't really noticed anything."

"You wouldn't," said Elwood. "It is outstanding for queer."

'If you don't mind, I'll slip out your back door and get busy with the competition," said Eddie.

Eddie smiled to himself as he came out of the alley. J.T. was obviously sending the counterfeit coins over here to his brother for him to pass to the unsuspecting. It was a good strategy, keeping the queer out of your own backyard. Eddie went down to the Silver Spur and worked the tables for a couple of hours. He left with some nice winnings, but nothing spectacular. Mary Helen was on his mind as he took the trolley line back to Cripple Creek. He grabbed his regular three newspapers and headed for the hotel to take it easy until their meeting.

CHAPTER 40

Kira got into town an hour before dusk with the wagon. She had two rifles, a pistol and a big skinning knife with her. She had left Nate at the cabin. He would just be in the way. It had taken some persuading, but she made his favorite dinner and promised she wouldn't be gone but a few hours. Nate wanted to go, but he hadn't liked it the night Kira had shot at that man. She had a strange gleam in her eyes now that scared him. When Kira got into town, she met Tom and Al at the Midland Train Terminal. She had picked that place because no one would notice another wagon, and they could blend in with the crowds.

As the brothers climbed into the wagon, Al exclaimed, "We did good, Kira! The Chinaman has a law office in Chinatown, but there is an alley next to the building where his office is," said Al. "We should be able to grab him there with no problem."

"What about Donnally?" she demanded.

"He's at the hotel reading a couple of newspapers as usual," said Tom. "But he went to the Golden Nugget in Victor."

"I knew the rat was onto J.T., and maybe even us. And the Haven House woman?" asked Kira.

"We're pretty sure she's in there. We asked around a little, and she spends most of her time there," said Al.

"Yeah, doing good deeds, I'll bet," said Kira, spitting in the dirt.

"How are you planning on doing this, Kira? You can't just stroll in and grab them," said Tom.

"You bet I can. I'm gonna walk in with my gun under this shawl. A gun in their ribs will make them do whatever I say," she said in a chilling tone.

"What do you want us to do?" asked Al.

"When I march them to the wagon, you two are going to make them lie down so you can hog tie and gag them. There are ropes and bandanas for gags under the tarp," she ordered.

Tom and Al exchanged glances.

"Don't worry about it. We will get it done so fast no one will notice," she barked, noticing their looks.

"Okay, Kira," they said practically together.

"Let's go get the Chinaman first," she said.

They drove down the main street of Chinatown, which was busy. There weren't many white people, but there were a few. It was just as Miss Mildred's girl had described. Kira drove around an adjacent building and then up the alley, stopping next to the stairs.

"You boys get the rope and tarp ready. I'll be right back," she said.

"This is crazy," hissed Al as Kira climbed the steps.

"I agree," said Tom, "but do you want to tell her that?"

Kira entered the office and shut the door. An Li had his back turned, putting a file away.

"Have a seat," said An Li, before turning.

Kira crossed the office in three strides and stuck her gun in An Li's back.

"I'm not sitting down, and neither are you," hissed Kira in a menacing tone.

"Whatever you say, Kira," answered An Li.

Him calling her name startled Kira, but her attention never wavered. She kept the gun jammed tight to An Li's spine.

"Let's go, now," she ordered, as she pushed him toward the door. They maneuvered down the steps, her gun never leaving his side. Tom and Al shoved An Li into the back of the wagon and quickly tied his hands behind him, bound his feet and gagged his mouth. After covering An Li with the tarp, the brothers jumped in the wagon and Kira pulled out into the street.

Gansulk was across the street and saw everything unfold. He had his bow and his quiver of arrows. He knew he could put an arrow in each of them, but the woman had the gun jammed right up against An Li. No matter where he hit her, the gun would probably go off. He also knew that killing three whites in the middle of Chinatown would be a disaster for his community. He had his horse and would follow. He knew his chance would come.

Kira drove the wagon up to the front of the Haven House as dusk was deepening. There was a slight knock on her office door, and Mary Helen said, "Come in," hoping it was Eddie arriving early. She stared as a large woman stepped in her office and pointed a pistol directly at her. "We don't have any money here," said Mary Helen.

"Shut up," snarled Kira. "I'm not here for money. Get up and step around your desk."

Recognition was coming to Mary Helen. "I know who you are," she blurted.

"Yeah, and I know who you are," sneered Kira, sticking the gun in Mary Helen's ribs hard enough to make her wince.

"We're going to walk out to the wagon in the street and you're not going to say a word to anyone," she ordered.

As Kira and Mary Helen started down the hall, Helene came out of a room behind them. She started to call out, but she could tell Kira had a gun stuck in Mary Helen's ribs. She froze until they turned the corner. Helene hurried to the corner and peeked around it in time to see Tom and Al load Mary Helen into the wagon. They tied and bound her just as they had An Li. Al and Tom jumped into the wagon and they moved away. Helene's mind was in a turmoil. Just as she started to go find Ellie, the three kids came in the door. Maggie took one look at her face and exclaimed, "What's happened?"

"A woman named Kira and her brothers just kidnapped Mary Helen. Have you seen Eddie?" blurted Helene.

"You stay here. We're going to Eddie's hotel," Stephen yelled as the trio took off at a run.

Kira drove the wagon to a side street next to the hotel. "You sure you don't want one of us to go with you?" asked Tom. Kira just glared and Tom held up his hands in submission. Kira walked up to the front desk and put one of her counterfeit gold pieces in front of the clerk.

"What room is Mr. Donnally in?" she asked, trying not to sound menacing.

The little man leaned forward and whispered the room number while putting the coin under the back of the book registry.

Eddie was adjusting his coat when there was a slight tap on his door. He opened it expecting An Li. Instead, it was Kira Cassidy with a large gun pointed directly at him.

"Step back and turn around," ordered Kira.

Eddie did as instructed. "I remember you from the trial now, Kira," he said.

"Shut up," she barked, and stuck the gun in Eddie's back.

"We're going downstairs and out the front door to the wagon. You're not saying a word to anyone if you want to live."

Eddie didn't have much choice but to do what he was told. Once in the street, his hands were quickly tied behind him, his feet bound and then he was gagged and roughly shoved under the tarp. He was horrified to be eye to eye with a very frightened Mary Helen, and by raising his head, could see An Li also tied and gagged behind her. At least they didn't have the kids he thought.

The wagon turned the corner and was out of sight just as the kids came running up the steps to the hotel. The pompous desk clerk yelled, "Stop. Your Uncle Eddie is not here."

"Did he leave with anybody?" asked Maggie, out of breath.

"He left with a rather large, unattractive woman," said the clerk condescendingly.

The trio turned away from the clerk and started across the lobby. "What do we do now?" asked Lizzie frightened as they passed the door to the hotel restaurant.

"Holy crap," exclaimed Stephen, stopping suddenly.

Maggie punched his arm and said, "You know you're not allowed to talk like that, Stephen."

"It's Will Scott," squeaked Lizzie.

"And Lisa," said Maggie, following their gaze.

"Maybe he can help," said Stephen, leading them into the restaurant and up to the table.

Lizzie spoke first, as usual. "Excuse me, Mr. Scott. You don't know us, but we are friends of Eddie Donnally, and we think he's in big trouble right now."

"What kind of trouble?" asked Will.

"He's been trying to catch some gold coin counterfeiters named Cassidy, and we think they just kidnapped him. The stupid desk clerk said he just left with a large, unattractive woman, and that fits Kira Cassidy's description. She's the leader of the counterfeit ring," finished Maggie.

"This is an emergency, Mr. Keegan," said Will as he and Lisa stood quickly, almost knocking the china cups over.

"We can finish up the claim paperwork tomorrow," said Lisa, as they headed for the front desk.

As they got to the front desk, Will practically shouted at the clerk, "We need to know exactly what you saw when Eddie Donnally left here."

The little man, seeing he was in a position of power began, "Sir, we do not . . ."

In one smooth motion, Will reached across the counter and grabbed the front of the man's shirt with one hand and snatched the man across the counter to within a foot of his own face. The smaller man's feet were off the floor dangling.

"Listen to me you little twit. I want to know everything you saw and heard, and I want to know it now," ordered Will.

"I saw Mr. Donnally crossing the lobby with this rather large, unattractive woman. They were walking very close together. She even had her arm linked through his," stammered the clerk.

"What was she wearing?" asked Will.

"Just a plain, common dress and a shawl," the clerk added.

"How did she know his room number?" asked Will.

The man glanced down at the gold piece that he had just put on the counter.

"Thank you," said Will, letting the man go. The man fell back off the counter, landing flat on his butt. Will pocketed the coin.

"Who is working with Eddie?" asked Will.

"An Li," said Maggie.

"Do you have any idea where he might be?" asked Will.

"Not really. We can go to Grandfather Chung's in Chinatown," said Lizzie. "I'm sure he can help."

Will turned toward Lisa, who was wearing a dress. "Why don't you go change and bring down our guns?"

Lisa pulled up her skirt and began running toward the stairs.

Will said, "I'll go outside and secure a cab. I think we have to hurry."

The kids just stood waiting and worrying until Lisa came back down the stairs. She had changed to jeans, shirt and boots. Her hair was pulled back, and she was carrying two rifles and a pistol belt. She had another pistol and holster around her waist.

The group rushed outside where Will was waiting at the curb with a taxi's carriage door open. They all clamored in, and Will said, "We need to go to Chinatown."

The driver turned and said, "You sure you want to go there at night, Mister?"

Will shoved a $20 double eagle toward the man. "Chinatown--as fast as you can get there."

The cab took off at a brisk pace. Lisa looked at the trio. "You seem to know us, but who are you?"

"I'm Maggie. Stephen and Lizzie are my cousins," she replied.

Will frowned. "I can't believe Eddie is using you in his case."

"It's kind of a long story. We better let Eddie explain," said Stephen.

"Fine," said Will. "Nice to meet you. We need to know as much as you can tell us about the case."

So, they quickly began telling Lisa and Will their story,

beginning with the results of the telegram, their planned meeting at Haven House, and ending up with Mary Helen's apparent kidnapping.

"We're in Chinatown," said the driver. "Where to, exactly?"

"To the pharmacy on Main Street," answered Stephen.

In a few moments, the cab stopped. The kids jumped out and headed for the door with Lisa close behind. Will tossed the cabbie another $20 gold piece and followed.

The door was unlocked and the lights were on. At the sound of the commotion, Grandfather Chung hurried out of the back room.

"What has happened?" he asked worriedly.

"Mary Helen and Eddie have been kidnapped. We need to see An Li," blurted out Stephen.

"Unfortunately, he has not been seen since late this afternoon," answered Chung.

"Great," said Will. "The Cassidy's have them, and we have no idea where."

"Not so," said Chung, holding up his hand. "One of my people knows the name, and we know where their cabin and mine are located. I am Chung."

"I'm Will Scott, and this is my wife, Lisa," said Will, answering the unspoken question.

Chung smiled, "You and Miguel are most revered. An Li and I have had long talks about the work of Secret Service Operatives."

"So, if you know where the Cassidy's are, we need to get moving," said Will. "Do you know the layout?"

"Come. I was just drawing it out," said Chung. "I did not know they had Eddie and the kind lady."

As they entered the back room, there was a Mongolian man

with a bow and notched arrow aimed directly at them. Chung said something in Chinese, and the man lowered his weapon.

"Here is, as you say, the layout. This is the cabin and there is a mine opening here. Unfortunately, they chose this place well. The only way in is this wagon trail here," informed Chung. "I'm sure they have An Li also."

"Do we know how many people are there?" asked Will. "I understand there are four in the family."

"That's right," spoke up Stephen. "But, Eddie and An Li believe J.T. Raines, the owner of the Wild Horse saloon, is in it with them. There are two really bad men, Powell and Braxton, who work for Raines."

"So, there's no way to know how many," complained Will.

"Not so," said Chung. "This is Bataar. At my request, his father has been following An Li without his knowledge. Gansulk is an expert horseman and a champion archer. I believe he will have followed them and is watching and waiting. He would have killed all three with his bow to protect An Li and the others if he could have."

"We can get close to their claim since the trail curves here," said Chung, pointing to his map.

"If I could borrow a horse and your man Bataar here, I'll . . .," started Will. Will stopped at the looks being given him by Lisa, the kids and Chung himself.

"You don't really think we should all go?" he asked in amazement.

"Way," said Stephen.

"What?" asked Will.

"You can either lead us and tell us what you want us to do, or get out of our way," insisted Maggie.

"They're right, Will," said Lisa. "We're not positive about the numbers, and we may need everyone."

"Do you kids know how to shoot?" asked Will.

"Yes sir. Our Abuelo taught us well, but rifles would be best," said Stephen.

Chung barked a few sentences in Chinese to Bataar and he hurried out. "Bataar has gone to get horses and rifles. He will be back shortly. How far ahead of us are they?"

"It seems Eddie was the last one they grabbed, so about 45 minutes now or so," answered Will. He took the coin from the hotel and looked at it in the light. "It's counterfeit, but it is really good. The whole Cassidy clan are all master counterfeiters."

There was a light tap on the rear door and Bataar entered carrying three rifles.

"Jeez, that was quick," said Stephen.

Bataar handed out the rifles and said something in Chinese to Chung.

"He says they are fully loaded," translated Chung.

Maggie, Stephen and Lizzie looked at the rifles, and then at Will. "We're familiar with this model," said Maggie. Abuelo was somewhat of a gun collector and the three had shot lever-action Winchesters plenty of times. Stephen had even taken a deer with one.

Chung went to a large cabinet and removed his own bow and quiver of arrows. "I am not as good as Gansulk and Bataar, but I have not forgotten how to use the bow," said Chung.

They all went outside and Bataar directed each of them to a horse.

Will looked at Chung. "You and Bataar should lead. I don't want an arrow in my ribs, since Gansulk doesn't know me."

"Very wise," said Chung, turning his horse and heading out at a fast clip.

The horses were on the small side, but their pace was smooth. The saddles Will assumed were Mongolian, and they were extremely comfortable. Will could tell the horses were not shod, and the reins were connected to a halter. There was nothing to creak or jangle. Lisa and I will have to look at these in the light, he thought. They rode hard for probably five miles and Will was amazed at what he could see of the landscape. It was vastly different from their ranch, since he saw almost no trees, just stumps. From what he could see, it was no wonder Lisa's dad had never wanted mining anywhere near the Cataloochee. The horses were blowing slightly when they stopped, but were obviously in good shape.

"This is the trail. We need to go single file from here," instructed Chung.

Lizzie started whispering to Maggie, "I'm a little nervous about shooting somebody. I've only shot targets. I haven't even hunted."

"Don't worry," replied Maggie. "I'm not crazy about having to shoot somebody either. Just aim over their heads and keep shooting. You can't go wrong that way. Will and the others will take care of the real shooting," she continued to whisper back at Lizzie.

CHAPTER 41

When Kira and her brothers got back to their claim, Kira jumped down quickly. "I've got to go check on Nate," she said.

"What do you want us to do with them?" asked Al, pointing to their prisoners.

"Nothing. Just leave them. They're not going anywhere," she laughed with that crazy gleam in her eyes. "I'll fix some supper and we'll have a celebration whisky."

Once Kira was in the house, Al turned to Tom. "Is she crazy, or what?"

"I think she is," said Tom. "Killing one Secret Service Operative, much less two, and a do-gooder woman, will unleash the hounds of hell on us."

"What are we going to do?" whispered Al.

"I think she is so far gone that she'd kill us too if we cross her," answered Tom. "After this is over, I think we should take all the bars and coins we can and head to Alaska," Tom continued. "We'll do whatever it takes to get away from Kira."

"Okay," said Al. "We might as well go in and eat and drink."

Under the tarp, all An Li, Mary Helen and Eddie could do was wait. As soon as Eddie and An Li were in the wagon, they had started doing Chinese meditation breathing techniques to keep their muscles relaxed and ready. Both believed at some point they would have an opportunity, and they intended to be ready.

Mary Helen was facing Eddie, and her eyes stayed locked on his despite being in a panic. She saw him start to modulate his breathing, and she could feel An Li on the other side of her doing the same thing. She started matching Eddie's breathing pattern and eventually felt herself relaxing despite their predicament. Then she realized circulation was returning to her bound limbs.

In the house, the first thing Kira did was console Nate. He had become scared and frantic when darkness came. Once she got him soothed, she started fixing supper, all the while softly singing an Irish folk tune.

"Why don't you get out the whisky, Tom?" she requested.

He got out the whisky and the glasses. He poured some whisky in two glasses. He and Al quickly threw them back feeling the burn.

"Hey, don't get started without me," said Kira jovially. "I told you boys my plan would work."

"It sure seems to," answered Tom.

CHAPTER 42

"How far up this trail?" asked Will.

"The driver who delivered firewood here said approximately one mile," answered Chung. "I expect Gansulk at that last curve."

They moved the horses rapidly for approximately half a mile then slowed to a walk. They were quiet, but you can only be so quiet with seven horses.

Bataar and Chung spoke in Chinese. "We should go on foot the rest of the way," informed Chung.

Will was third in line in front of the kids with Lisa bringing up the rear. As they neared the final curve in the trail, a shadow appeared between Bataar and Chung and spoke in soft Chinese. Will thought himself observant, but the man just appeared. Lizzie gave a little squeak. The group gathered around Bataar, Chung and Gansulk.

"Gansulk speaks English," said Chung, "but is better in Chinese." Chung quietly introduced them all.

Gansulk squatted in the sand and drew out the claim. There was just enough moonlight to see. Thank goodness its not a full moon, thought Will.

"The house is here, and the wagon is in front," Chung translated. "I think our friends are still unharmed, but tied up in the wagon. They will probably take them into the mine. Perhaps we can get to the wagon first. There are large boulders up to about 50 yards off the house. The mine opening sits here, and they must do something in the mine since our man unloaded a stack of wood near the mouth. I recommend Bataar and I take up positions right and left."

Gansulk pointed to Will, and with Chung translating, continued, "You and grandfather can work your way up to the wagon and free them if you can. We will cover you. If they go to the mine before we can get there, you can take cover behind the wood pile and cover the center." Pointing to the three kids and Lisa, he said, "You should fan out and take up positions here," making a half moon in the dirt. "You should be in the middle," he said, pointing to Lisa.

Chung looked at Will, who said, "It looks like the perfect plan to me, almost. If we can get to the wagon, it would be great. If we don't get to the wagon in time, we need to lure some of them out of the mine, if possible. But, we will have to see. Maybe one of them will come out to relieve themselves."

Chung translated to Bataar and Gansulk, and both men smiled.

Holding up his hand, Will said, "We need to take them alive if possible. If we hear any screams, I'll rush the mine entrance, and you follow. Unfortunately, we probably need to hurry."

Chung translated, and both men nodded. Bataar and Gansulk vanished, heading for their positions. The other five spread out and moved forward.

Lisa stepped to Will and grabbed his hand. "I can't make it without you, so please be careful."

"I promise," said Will. "You too, okay?"

Halfway to their spots, the cabin door opened and Kira and her brothers walked down to the wagon.

The rescue party froze, but they were all concealed by the

darkness and boulders. In addition, the Cassidy's were concentrating solely on their prisoners.

"Cut their feet free, Al. We're not carrying this scum," sneered Kira.

Al removed the gags as well.

From his spot, Will could see that Kira had a knife in one hand and a pistol in the other. Tom had a pistol and a rifle, while Al only had a pistol and a belt knife.

"Start walking toward the mine, scum," Kira ordered. She sheathed her knife, grabbed Mary Helen's arm and stuck the pistol in her ribs. "Just in case these boys get frisky," she said, as she marched them into the mine.

When the Cassidys entered the mine, Lisa and the kids moved into position. There is no going back now thought Lisa. She could barely see Chung and Will as they moved forward and crouched behind the wood pile.

Inside the mine, Kira kept her pistol on the trio as Al and Tom lit several kerosene lanterns. The lanterns made the cave almost daylight bright. They went around a turn and stopped in a large room cut into the wall off the main tunnel.

"Sit down against that wall you scum," bellowed Kira.

Eddie and An Li could see this was where Kira did her work. There were dies and engraving tools in plain sight on the work table. In one corner of the room was what looked like maybe 100 gold bars, sitting on a pallet. There were multiple stacks of gold coins on another table.

"So, what do you think of my place Mr. Secret Service Operatives?" snarled Kira. She gave Mary Helen's outstretched leg a kick hard enough to illicit a moan.

"Leave her alone, Kira. She's not an operative," said Eddie.

"No, but I can tell she means something to you. What do

you think, Mr. Chinaman? Ever seen anything like this?" Kira said, sweeping her arm around.

"No," said An Li. "I can see why your counterfeits are so good, Kira."

"I learned from the best, you know, my Uncle Tom. But Mr. stinking Eddie Donnally there put him in prison. Start a little fire over there in the corner Al. I want to heat up my knife a little." She held up her knife and it gleamed in the lights from the lanterns. "You're going to get to know this blade real well, little girlie," said Kira, giving Mary Helen's leg another kick.

Mary Helen clenched her teeth to keep from crying out.

Eddie and An Li could both see the insanity in Kira's eyes.

"How's that fire coming, Al?" Kira asked.

"It's coming along. Just taking a little time to get the coals hot," he answered.

"Tom, why don't you go back and get the whisky so I can celebrate while I'm having fun," instructed Kira.

"Okay, anything you say," replied Tom.

"Damn right," said Kira to no one in particular, as she paced in front of the prisoners.

Tom got outside and took a breath of clean air. Jeez, he thought to himself, I'd like to just jump on my horse and go. It was the last thought he had as Will's fist crunched into his jaw, knocking him out cold.

Chung alertly grabbed the rifle before it hit the ground. Chung pulled two lengths of rope and a bandanna out of the pocket of his Chinese robe. At Will's astonished look, he whispered, "Confucius say, always be prepared."

It was all Will could do not to bust out laughing, despite the circumstances.

Chung expertly tied Tom Cassidy up and gagged him, just

in case.

Inside the mine, Kira was ranting and raving as she described what she was going to do to Mary Helen in front of Eddie. "Maybe I'll scalp her like the Indians used to do. Maybe I'll cut her face so bad, kids will run from her. What is Tom doing? How long does it take to get a bottle?" she asked rhetorically. "Go check on him, Al. He may have gotten squeamish on me. I bet he'd rush right back if I let him have his way with Miss Goody-two-shoes here."

Eddie saw an opening, and said," Did you set all this up yourself, Kira?"

She turned toward him. "Of course I did. Those two fool brothers of mine helped a little. Or I should say, did what I told them to do."

Al came to the mouth of the tunnel and looked out, searching the night for Tom. "Tom," he called. I hope he didn't get on his horse and ride thought Al. Kira was scaring even him. He took another half dozen steps away from the tunnel trying to see their horses but stopped short of Will. Will felt rather than saw Chung raise his hand. In a blur, two arrows came out of the night. One struck Al in the side right between his ribs and lodged in his heart. The second hit him in the neck in a downward trajectory. He's dead twice, even before he hit the ground, thought Will.

Meanwhile, in the mine, Kira continued her rants and pacing. She had the knife in one hand and the gun in the other. There was spittle around her mouth and she looked even wilder, if that was possible.

Will and Chung moved up to the mouth of the tunnel. Will had his gun out, and Chung had an arrow notched. They could hear Kira's rants. Will pointed to the floor of the tunnel. It was covered with loose stones. There was no way anyone was going down the tunnel undetected.

At that moment, Nate came out on the porch carrying a rifle. "Kira," he yelled, "there are . . .

It was as far as he got. Chung whirled, pulling back his bow and sending an arrow straight into Nate's chest. He fell without a sound, but his rifle made a loud clatter.

At the call from Nate, Kira stopped her rants. "Al, Tom, what the hell is going on out there?" she called. When she got no response, she moved to the room's doorway. If there's anyone else out there, don't come in unless you want me to kill these three."

Will looked at Chung and shrugged. He was going to try to distract her and maybe Eddie and An Li could do something. Will knew they were just waiting for an opening.

"Kira," Will shouted into the mine opening.

"It's me, Will Scott. You remember me?"

"I remember you!" screamed Kira. "You're as bad as this scum in here. I heard you quit and came out West. I should have known it was just another lie."

"Kira, we have this place surrounded, and your brothers are in custody. Give it up before someone gets hurt," called Will.

Kira stuck the hand with the pistol out and fired three shots toward the tunnel mouth. "That's what I think of you and your scum out there," she called. "I'm going to shoot Miss Goody-two-shoes in here just to show you I mean business."

While Will had distracted Kira, Eddie and An Li had both slid down the wall to more evenly distribute their weight.

Kira walked over and stood in front of Eddie and said, "Say goodbye to your little sweetie, Donnally." She was pointing the gun straight at Mary Helen. Kira turned her head and yelled back at Will. "The next sound you hear will be someone dying."

Before Kira could turn back, Eddie kicked with everything he had at the back of her knees. He could feel tendons and ligaments tear. She screamed and with her weight, fell back flat on her butt. At the same instant, An Li launched a kick that caught her square in the back of the head, slamming her chin down to her breastbone. The gun and knife fell from her hands as she slowly toppled over.

"Will," called Eddie. "She's down. It's safe. It's not a trick. She didn't count on our feet."

Will and Chung charged down the tunnel and into the side room.

"You are a sight for sore eyes," blurted Eddie.

Will picked up Kira's knife and gun. He quickly cut all three prisoners loose.

"Good to see you again, An Li. I warned you about working with a crazy Irishman," joked Will.

Kira moaned.

"I can't wait for her to come around. She is going to have a giant headache," said An Li, laughing.

By now, all the rescuers had reached the mine and were now crowded into the room.

"What happened?" asked Lizzie.

"Kira made the mistake of not binding their feet. Their kung fu practices came in handy," said Chung.

"We knew what we wanted to do, but she wouldn't stand still," said Eddie. "She kept pacing back and forth."

"She is truly a raving lunatic," added a shivering Mary Helen, who was being hugged tightly by Eddie.

"Regrettably, two of her brothers are dead," sighed Chung.

"The retarded one?" asked Mary Helen questioningly.

"He came out on the porch with a rifle. We had no choice. I was pulling the trigger, but an arrow got there first," said Lisa.

Mary Helen blinked back tears for Nate.

"It's alright Mary Helen. We are all safe now," said Eddie, trying to comfort her.

"Wow!" exclaimed Stephen. "Look at all this gold. There's a fortune here."

"It's all counterfeit, you dipstick," said Maggie. "Besides, it's all evidence now."

"Bataar and Gansulk will bury the dead. I will say a prayer for their souls," said Chung. "It is very important that no one knows they were killed by members of the Chinese community.

Photo, Counterfeit Coin Plant, circa 1900,
(courtesy Mike Sampson, Archivist, U.S. Secret Service.)

Even though it was justified, there are many who would use it as an excuse to cause serious trouble."

"We all understand," said Eddie. "By the way, excuse me, Mrs. Scott, may I present Miss Mary Helen McDougal."

"Good to meet you," said Lisa. "C'mere you," and she gave Eddie a big hug. "I'm glad to see you."

"We've still got a lot of work to do," said An Li. "Grandfather, do you think you could get people from Chinatown to guard this mine?"

"It would be our honor. Consider it done," said Chung.

"Who else do we have to get?" asked Will.

"J.T. Raines, the owner of the Wild Horse Saloon and Gambling Hall. He has two thugs, Braxton and Powell who we need to nab also," said Eddie. "I think Kira just went crazy with rage and I don't think they have any idea we're coming for them."

"Don't forget the brother in Victor," added Mary Helen.

"You guys have been busy," said Will. "This operation rivals any we had back East."

It took four of them to load Kira into the wagon and get her tied up. She moaned a little, but still didn't come around. Tom was awake, but a little groggy.

"Let's take these two to the town Marshal's jail," said Eddie. "I've got a way to snare J.T. and his boys," he added.

Chung led the way back to town and then broke off to arrange more guards to relieve Bataar and Gansulk.

They deposited the prisoners at the jail. Eddie said, "Lisa, would you and the kids mind sending a telegram to Washington? Tell them we have multiple defendants, and the U.S. Marshal's Office in Denver needs to bring a transport wagon. If you could, also send a message to the Denver Secret

Service Office telling them the plant is suppressed. Ask them to send a troop detachment to transport evidence. It would probably be best to use the telegraph office at the Midland Terminal."

"Listen, Eddie," said Mary Helen. "I'm going to Haven House, unless you need me. I'm sure they are worried sick about me."

"I'm going with you Mary Helen, if that's okay. I'm worn out," said Lizzie.

"Of course," said Mary Helen. "I'll have a big breakfast ready for everyone in the morning." Mary Helen's eyes and Eddie's hardly left each other.

After Mary Helen and Lizzie left, Lisa turned to Eddie. "You got it bad."

The kids just stared.

"What!" exclaimed Eddie.

"I second that motion," said An Li.

"Thanks," said Eddie. "You're supposed to be my partner."

An Li started, "Confucius say . . .

"I don't want to hear it," said Eddie. "Let's get to work and quit the chatter."

CHAPTER 43

Eddie strolled into the Wild Horse looking for J.T. The place was hopping. It looked like every table was full. Eddie spotted J.T. and pushed his way through the crowd.

Eddie leaned in close, "Let's talk in your office. I've got some good news."

J.T. led Eddie to his office. Once inside, J.T. turned his back on Eddie to lock the door. When he turned back, Eddie had a gun in his hand.

"What the . . ." started J.T.

"Shut up and sit at your desk," ordered Eddie.

Keeping his gun trained on J.T., Eddie unlocked the alley door. An Li and Will stepped inside. An Li had his pistol out. Will carried a holstered pistol and a sawed off double-barrel he had borrowed from the town Marshal. An Li had his Secret Service badge pinned to his chest, while Will had Eddie's pinned to his.

"You're under arrest, J.T., for violating the counterfeiting laws of the United States," said Eddie.

An Li snapped cuffs on J.T.'s wrists, securing him to the arm of his chair.

"I'm sure he's got at least one hideout gun on him," said Eddie.

"Make that two," said An Li, removing a pistol from under

J.T.'s arm and a derringer from his vest pocket.

"Braxton and Powell are on the floor now, and I'm sure they saw me and J.T.," said Eddie. "There should be no problem getting them in here." He went back out on the floor and found the two thugs.

"J.T. wants to see you in his office," said Eddie.

Braxton went in first, with Powell following. Eddie gave Powell a hard shove in the back. They both stumbled, and when they looked up, they were looking down gun barrels the wrong way. Seeing the Secret Service badges, both raised their hands.

"You two are under arrest for violating the counterfeiting laws of the United States. Also, on suspicion regarding the murder of Jeremiah Klein," said Eddie.

"Hey, that wasn't our idea," blurted Powell. "J.T. told us to."

"Shut up you fool," barked J.T.

The two were handcuffed, and along with J.T., quickly taken to the town jail.

"You boys want to see Victor?" asked Eddie.

Before they could reply, Lisa, Maggie and Stephen walked up to the Marshal's office. "Did you get them?" asked Stephen.

"Yes, and with no hitches," answered An Li. "It helped having Will with us. None of the three of them even had a clue. Kira had obviously not told them anything."

"We need to go to Victor and pick him up one more suspect and some counterfeit coins," said Will, looking at Lisa.

"I understand. Why don't I escort these two back to Mary Helen and check on her?" asked Lisa. "I'll meet you back at the hotel a little later."

"Thanks," said Eddie and Will simultaneously.

The two groups then went their separate ways. Even

Stephen and Maggie had experienced enough excitement for one day.

In Victor, Eddie and An Li enlisted the town Marshal and three deputies to help them. Eddie lured J.T.'s brother into his own office and stuck a gun in his face just as before. The Marshal, three deputies, An Li and Will came in the alley door. The Marshal had agreed to shut down the Golden Nugget and collect all the money off the floor.

"You're under arrest for violating the counterfeiting laws of the United States," said Eddie. "Look, Elwood, you know you are in big trouble. We'd appreciate it if you would just tell us where the money is hidden. J.T. and his boys are already in jail."

"Okay," said Elwood, caving easily. "Will you tell the judge I helped? And I didn't have anything to do with that Klein fella."

"It will be in our report," said An Li.

With Elwood's help, they quickly recovered two bags of counterfeit gold coins and two bags of genuine coins. The Marshal and his deputies came in with two more bags off the floor.

"How did it go?" asked An Li.

"Soon as we told them that they were all getting paid with counterfeit money, they all turned the money over. The whole bunch was getting real surly with the dealers. I'm going to have to leave the deputies here to stop a lynching," laughed the Marshal.

"Could we put these bags in your safe, Marshal?" asked Eddie.

"Of course," he answered.

"It shouldn't be more than a day or so," said An Li.

After stowing the money safely in the Marshal's safe, the

three men caught the short train back to Cripple Creek.

"I'm headed to Chinatown and some rest," said An Li, once they reached the terminal.

"We'll see you at 10:00 o'clock in the morning at Mary Helen's, partner," answered Eddie.

Eddie and Will walked back to the hotel all the while talking.

"By the way, how's Miguel?" asked Eddie.

"Let's just say I think you will have another wedding to come out to before long," replied Will. "I guess I better give you this back," he continued, reluctantly handing Eddie back his badge.

"Do you miss it, Will?" asked Eddie.

"Sometimes I think I do, but then I look at Lisa and I know I'm where I'm supposed to be," answered Will. "Lisa and An Li are right, pal. You do have it bad," he chuckled.

"I guess I do," sighed Eddie. "But, I just can't see a future in it."

"Talk to Mary Helen," said Will. "Maybe you can figure out a way to make it work together."

A short time later, Will let himself into his room and wasn't surprised to see Lisa waiting up for him.

"How did it go?" she asked.

"Easy. The town Marshal helped out, and we just secured all the money in his safe," answered Will.

Will slipped into bed beside Lisa and knew he was home.

Lisa said, "You know, in Leadville, I was terrified, but you saved us. Tonight, being on your side was exciting despite the danger. I can see why you, Miguel, Eddie and An Li do the job. Do you miss it?"

"Sometimes I do, but it's a little like a pleasant memory of something in your past," answered Will, turning out the light. "I don't want to do anything else but what we are about to do right now."

The next morning, everyone showed up at Mary Helen's as scheduled. Eddie had a fist full of telegrams, which he gladly shared with An Li.

"Looks like you fellas got some work to do," laughed Will.

"You never said why you and Miss Lisa were here in Cripple Creek," interjected Maggie.

"My dad was a mining engineer, and besides finding and staking claims for some big syndicates, he claimed a few for himself. That lawyer you saw us with is offering an absurdly large amount of money for one of them," explained Lisa. "By the way, Mary Helen, you can expect a large donation to Haven House when this deal goes through."

"Thank you, Lisa. We need all the help we can get. There's always a need here," answered Mary Helen.

Lisa was just about to ask the trio about themselves, but Ellie and a helper brought out platters of food. She put one plate of food in front of Eddie and said, "with."

"With or without rat poison," explained Eddie, blushing.

Will and Lisa howled.

Eddie scowled and said, "If you think it's so funny, you eat it."

"I'll take it," said Mary Helen, moving the plate in front of her.

Ellie saw it from the kitchen and rushed over to take the plate from in front of Mary Helen. Then, she burst out laughing herself and gave Eddie a wink.

"See how they treat me around here," grumbled Eddie, locking eyes with Mary Helen.

After eating until they were stuffed, Lisa and Will rushed off to finish their meeting with the lawyer.

An Li asked, "You kids want to visit Grandfather Chung with me?"

"Sure," they replied in unison, all three sneaking peaks at Eddie and Mary Helen.

"You guys did a fine job last night. I guess the little man was right. We needed a wee bit of help," said Eddie. "C'mere," he said, and gave them each a big hug. "You three are officially Irish!" Eddie exclaimed, and An Li and Mary Helen smiled.

"Why don't we go to my office, Eddie?" asked Mary Helen.

As soon as Eddie shut the office door, Mary Helen threw herself into his arms. They kissed for what seemed like a lifetime. When they parted, Eddie was speechless.

"Top of the morning, Mr. Donnally," said Mary Helen.

"Listen, Mary Helen, I really like you, and I guess you like me a little," stammered Eddie. "But, you know I'm going back to New York in a few days."

"What makes you think I'm not going with you?" asked Mary Helen. "If you want me to, that is."

"Don't you have to stay here?" he asked, incredulously.

"No. I don't. I told you before I'm not a nun," replied Mary Helen. "Haven House is a big charity, and I'm a paid employee. They have a place for me in New York. I was never going to stay here permanently. It will take me a little while to train her, but I think Helene can handle this place. Besides, she has a history here, and the girls on Meyers Avenue will respect her. Most of them just call me 'Miss goody-two-shoes'."

"Top of the morning yourself," said Eddie, pulling her close for another kiss to seal the deal.

While Eddie and Mary Helen were working out their future together, An Li and the kids shared tea with Grandfather Chung.

"I know you kids are not from here, but those tokens I gave you are good anywhere," said Chung.

"Thank you," said Maggie, speaking for all of them.

The doorbell tinkled and Chung excused himself.

An Li looked at them seriously. He held up three train tickets. "These showed up on my dresser this morning."

"So, I guess we're leaving," said Stephen, glumly.

"You know, you three did an outstanding job helping us," said An Li. "I talked to Eddie. We both agree that we're truly sorry to see you leave."

"Do you think Eddie and Mary Helen will end up together?" asked Maggie.

Chung, coming back in, had overheard the question, and said with a big smile, "I predict many years of happiness."

EPILOGUE

An Li walked with them to the train terminal. They all hugged An Li, and a tear or two escaped from Maggie and Lizzie, while Stephen blinked a lot. They didn't bother getting their clothes at the Haven House.

"All aboard," shouted the Conductor.

Lisa and Will were in the hotel packing, and Lisa said, "Those kids were something. Where did they come from anyway?"

I asked Eddie, and he started to talk, but then just stopped and shrugged his shoulders," replied Will.

"I'll ask him and An Li at lunch and see what I can get out of them," grinned Lisa.

Will just rolled his eyes. "I don't know why or how, but it felt like those kids knew me and I knew them," replied Will. "But, I agree with An Li, they do talk funny."

"Hey!" exclaimed Lisa. "I felt the same way. Maybe it will come to us. Their parents whoever or wherever should be proud of them. I was glad none of them had to shoot anyone."

On the train, the conductor took the trio's tickets on the Thunder Canyon Bridge just before the tunnel. They could hear the almost continuous dynamite blasts just as before. But, as they came out of the tunnel, they were speeding along on the Thunder Mountain ride in Walt Disney World.

Mimi met them as they came off the ride.

"We had a great trip, Mimi," said Lizzie.

"Yeah," said Stephen.

"Thanks for letting us go," added Maggie.

Mimi just smiled. "Abuelo is holding a table for us over at the Crystal Palace. You can tell us all about it."

Abuelo had gotten a table in one corner away from the crowd. The kids told their adventure from beginning to end, leaving nothing out.

"We didn't like it when we had to leave," said Maggie.

"We have no idea what happened with Mary Helen and Eddie," said Lizzie, frowning.

"You know," said Abuelo, "there are a lot of records available if you three want to do some historical research. Don't you usually have a special project over the Christmas break?"

"Is it on a computer?" asked Stephen.

"I believe it is," answered Abuelo, laughing.

"You kidding?" asked Maggie. "We're not waiting that long. We'll get to work on it as soon as we get home."

Stephen and Lizzie nodded their agreement.

"Did you guys bring back any souvenirs this time?" asked Mimi.

"No," answered Stephen. "Wait, I feel something in my pocket."

The other two dug in their pockets as well. All three produced a bronze coin with a Chinese character and a dragon.

"Cool," said Stephen. "These are not glowing, and they are the exact ones we got from Grandfather."

"That's quite a surprise," said Mimi.

"Maybe you can research the coin and Chinese letter too. Those medallions look very old and may mean something," added Abuelo. "I'll get each of you a chain so you can wear them around your neck. I'm sure the only thing you will be able to say about them is that they were a gift."

"I like it," said Stephen. "I just wish I could have brought back my shillelagh."

Two weeks later, both families were at Mimi and Abuelo's for dinner. After dinner, the kids were alone with Mimi.

"Stephen, this package came for you," she said. "It doesn't have a return address."

Stephen tore into the package and proudly pulled out the shillelagh that had felled Kira. "Now this is what I call a perfect ending," he beamed.

The girls just rolled their eyes.

APPENDIX A

Faro: The most popular card game in the Old West

Faro, Pharaoh, or Farobank, is a late 17th-century French gambling card game descendant of basset, and belongs to the lansquenet and Monte Bank family of games, in that it is played between a banker and several players winning or losing according to the cards turned up matching those already exposed or not.

Although not a direct relative of poker, faro was played by the masses alongside its other popular counterpart, due to its fast action, easy-to-learn rules, and better odds than most games of chance. The game of faro is played with only one deck of cards and allows for any number of players.

MEN PLAYING FARO IN AN ARIZONA SALOON IN 1895

France

The earliest references to a card game named pharaoh are found in Southwestern France during the reign of Louis XIV. Basset was outlawed in 1691, and pharaoh emerged several years later as a derivative of basset, before it too was outlawed.

United States

With its name shortened to faro, it soon spread to the United States in the 19th century to become the most widespread and popularly favored gambling game. It was played in almost every gambling hall in the Old West from 1825 to 1915. Faro could be played in over 150 places in Washington, DC alone during the Civil War. An 1882 study considered faro to be the most popular form of gambling, surpassing all other forms combined in terms of money wagered each year.

The faro game was also called "bucking the tiger" or "twisting the tiger's tail", which comes from early card backs that featured a drawing of a Bengal tiger. By the mid-19th century, the tiger was so commonly associated with the game that gambling districts where faro was popular became known as "tiger town", or in the case of smaller venues, "tiger alley". In fact, some gambling houses would simply hang a picture of a tiger in their windows to advertise that a game could be found within.

Faro's detractors regarded it as a dangerous scam that destroyed families and reduced men to poverty because of rampant rigging of the dealing box. Crooked faro equipment was so popular that many sporting-house companies began to supply gaffed dealing boxes specially designed so that the bankers could cheat their players. Cheating was prevalent enough that editions of Hoyle's Rules of Games began their faro section warning readers that not a single honest faro bank could be found in the United States. While the game became scarce after World War II, it continued to be played at a few Las Vegas and Reno casinos through 1985.

Criminal prosecutions of faro were involved in the Supreme Court cases of United States v. Simms, 5 U.S. (1 Cranch) 252 (1803), and Ex parte Milburn, 34 U.S. (9 Pet.) 704 (1835).

Description

A game of faro was often called a "faro bank". It was played with an entire deck of playing cards. One person was designated the "banker" and an indeterminate number of players, known as "punters", could be admitted. Chips (called "checks") were purchased by the punter from the banker (or house) from which the game originated. Bet values and limits were set by the house. Usual check values were 50 cents to $10 each.

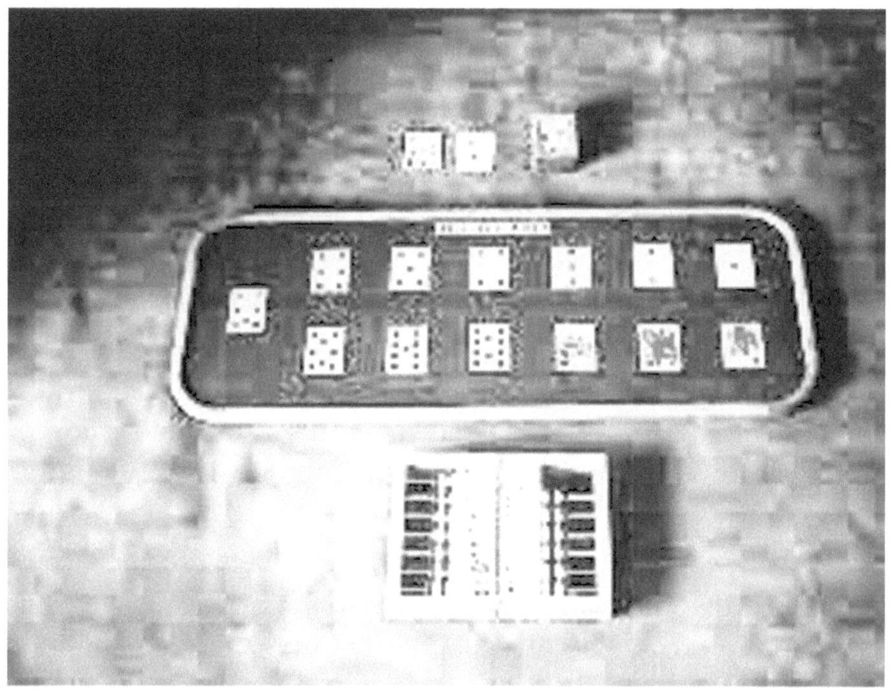

THE LAYOUT OF A FARO BOARD.

The faro table was typically oval, covered with green baize, and had a cutout for the banker. A board with a standardized betting layout consisting of all cards of one suit pasted to it in numerical order, called the "layout", was placed on top of the table. Traditionally, the suit of spades was used for the layout. Each player laid his stake on one of the 13 cards on the layout. Players could place multiple bets and could bet on multiple cards simultaneously by placing their bet between cards or on specific card edges. Players also had the choice of betting on the "high card" bar located at the top of the layout.

Procedure

- A deck of cards was shuffled and placed inside a "dealing box", a mechanical device also known as a "shoe", which was used to prevent manipulations of the draw by the banker and intended to assure players of a fair game.
- The first card in the dealing box was called the "soda" and was "burned off", leaving 51 cards in play. The dealer then drew 2 cards: the first was called the "banker's card" and was placed on the right side of the dealing box. The next card after the banker's card was called the carte Anglaise (English card) or simply the "player's card", and it was placed on the left of the shoe.
- The banker's card was the "losing card". All bets placed on that card were lost by the players and won by the bank. The player's card was the "winning card". All bets placed on that card were returned to the players with a 1 to 1 (even money) payout by the bank (e.g. a dollar bet won a dollar). A "high card" bet won if the player's card had a higher value than the banker's card. The dealer settled all bets after each two cards drawn. This allowed players to bet before drawing the next two cards. Bets that neither won nor lost remained on the table, and could be picked up or changed by the player prior to the next draw.
- A player could reverse the intent of his bet by placing a hexagonal (6-sided) token called a "copper" on it. Some

histories said a penny was sometimes used in place of a copper. This was known as "coppering" the bet, and reversed the meaning of the win/loss piles for that particular bet.

- When only 3 cards remained in the dealing box, the dealer would "call the turn", which was a special type of bet that occurred at the end of each round. The object now was to predict the exact order that the 3 remaining cards, Bankers, Players, and the final card called the Hock, would be drawn. The player's odds here were 5 to 1, while a successful bet paid off at 4 to 1 (or 1 to 1 if there were a pair among the 3, known as a "cat-hop"). This provided one of the dealer's few advantages in faro. If it happened that the 3 remaining cards were all the same, there would be no final bet, as the outcome was not in question.

A device, called a "casekeep" was employed to assist the players and prevent dealer cheating by counting cards. The casekeeper resembled an abacus, with one spindle for each card denomination. As a card was played, either winning or losing, one of 4 counters would be moved to indicate that it had been played. This allowed players to plan their bets by keeping track of what cards remained available in the dealing box. The operator of the casekeep is called the "casekeeper", or colloquially in the American West, the "coffin driver".

Certain advantages were reserved to the banker: if he drew a doublet, that is, two equal cards, he won half of the stakes upon the card which equaled the doublet. In a fair game, this provided the only "house edge". If the banker drew the last card of the pack, he was exempt from doubling the stakes deposited on that card. These and the advantage from the odds on the turn bet provided a slight financial advantage to the dealer or house. To give themselves more of an advantage, and to counter the losses from players cheating, the dealers would also often cheat as well.

Cheating

In a fair game, the house's edge was low, so bankers increasingly resorted to cheating the players to increase the profitability of the game for the house. This too was acknowledged by Hoyle editors when describing how faro banks were opened and operated: "To justify the initial expenditure, a dealer must have some permanent advantage."

Being caught cheating often resulted in a fight, or even gunfire.

By dealers

Dealers employed several methods of cheating:

- Stacked or rigged decks: A stacked deck would consist of many paired cards, allowing the dealer to claim half of the bets on that card, as per the rules. A rigged deck would contain textured cards that allowed dealers to create paired cards in the deck while giving the illusion of thorough shuffling.

- Rigged dealing boxes: Rigged, or "gaffed", dealing boxes came in several variants. Typically, they allowed the dealer to see the next card prior to the deal, by use of a small mirror or prism visible only to the dealer. If the next card was heavily bet, the box could also allow the dealer to draw 2 cards in one draw, thus hiding the card that would have paid. This would result in the casekeeper not accounting for the hidden card, however. If the casekeeper were employed by the house, though, he could take the blame for "accidentally" not logging that card when it was drawn.

- Sleight of hand: In concert with the rigged dealing box, the dealer could, when he knew the next card to win, surreptitiously slide a player's bet off of the winning card if it was on the dealer's side of the layout. At a hectic faro table, he could often get away with this, though it was obviously a risky move if caught.

By players

Players would routinely cheat as well. Their techniques employed distraction and sleight-of-hand, and usually involved moving their stake to a winning card, or at the very least, off of the losing card, without being detected. Their methods ranged from crude to creative, and worked best at a busy, fast-paced table:

- Simple move of their bet: The most basic cheat was simply to move one's bet to the adjacent card on the layout while avoiding the banker noticing. While the simplest, it also carried the greatest risk of detection.

- Moving with a thread: A silk thread or single horse hair would be affixed to the bottom check in the bet, and allowed the stack to be pulled across the table to another card on the layout. This was less risky, as the cheating player would not have to make an overt action.

- Removing the copper: A variant on the use of the thread was to affix it to the copper token used to reverse the bet. If the losing card matched the player's bet, the copper made it a winning bet and no cheat was needed. If, however, the winning card, dealt second, were to match the player's bet the copper would ordinarily make it a loser, but quickly snatching the copper from the stack with the invisible thread turned it into a winner. This held the least risk, as once the copper was yanked from the stack, there was no thread left attached to the bet.

More information about Faro Card Game may be found at http://en.wikipedia.org/wiki/Faro_(card_game)

- Title: Worthy of Trust and Confidence™
- Author: Donald Brewer
- Publisher: TotalRecall Publications, Inc.
- Format:
  Hardcover,   ISBN: 9781590950548
  Paperback,   ISBN: 9781590950555
  eBook,   ISBN: 9781590950562
  Audio Book,   ISBN: 9781590952597

A trio of cousins researching a family history project encounter a leprechaun who gives them a secret service badge to a Magical Mousegate. The Mousegate is in Walt Disney World and will transport them to an old West Secret Service counterfeiting case.

The trio is embedded with the consciousness of the three main characters in the western action novel, and follow the case from beginning to end while experiencing life through their characters' eyes, hearts and minds.

While the Prologue and Epilogue detail the actions of the teens, the rest of the book is a classic old style Western mystery. There are bank robbers, crooked politicians, a love interest, and a shootout.

The book would be enjoyable for early to mid-teen readers, boys and girls alike, as well as adults. It is an unusual adventure, since it details the actions of Secret Service operatives while investigating counterfeit currency in the Old West in 1898.

Worthy of Trust and Confidence, was one of the three finalists in the Colorado Authors League, Young Adult Book of the Year for 2014 and Grand Prize winner in The Ultimate Heroes Writing Contest, Western Division.

A Mouse Gate Adventure Book

What's your adventure?